D0094162

MY DEAREST NANCY

Travelling north, Nancy meets a young soldier. It's 1939 and Great Britain is on the brink of war. The soldier leaves the train and Nancy finds a letter he'd started to write — just three words: *My Dearest Nancy*... Then, two years later, working as a nurse, she meets him again, but he's wounded and apparently blinded. She finds herself falling in love with him, but could he recover from his injuries — and the betrayal of the other Nancy?

*Books by Marlene E. McFadden
in the Linford Romance Library:*

PATH OF TRUE LOVE
TOMORROW ALWAYS COMES
WHEN LOVE IS LOST
EACH TIME WE MEET

MARLENE E. McFADDEN

MY DEAREST NANCY

Complete and Unabridged

LINFORD
Leicester

First published in Great Britain in 2007

First Linford Edition
published 2008

British Library CIP Data

McFadden, Marlene E. (Marlene Elizabeth), 1937 –
    My dearest Nancy.—Large print ed.—
    Linford romance library
    1. Love stories
    2. Large type books
    I. Title
    823.9'14 [F]

    ISBN 978–1–84782–376–2

Published by
F. A. Thorpe (Publishing)
Anstey, Leicestershire

Set by Words & Graphics Ltd.
Anstey, Leicestershire
Printed and bound in Great Britain by
T. J. International Ltd., Padstow, Cornwall

This book is printed on acid-free paper

1

Nancy wasn't sure now that she was on her way home that she shouldn't have worn her black coat instead of this light linen jacket and summery hat, but she hated herself in black and there would be time enough for that at the funeral.

She turned her head to look out of the window of the moving train. They were well away from London by now, journeying through gentle fields and rolling hills. She thought about Hepplestone, the small Yorkshire market town where she had been born, where her father had been the local doctor for many years.

Her eyes filled with tears. She couldn't really believe even now that he had died. It had been so sudden, a telegram had arrived informing her that Dr John Mellor had suffered a fatal heart attack. There had been no warning.

She had made arrangements immediately to take time off work; her employer, Mr Plummer, the manager of Randalls, a plush departmental store in Kingston-on-Thames where she worked as a nurse, had told her in a kindly voice, 'Take all the time you need, Nancy. We'll manage. You're an excellent employee and of course you must go home.' He took hold of her hand, patting her fingers, 'Things are difficult at the moment, for everyone. Will there be a war, won't there be a war, but family must come first. I know you must be deeply shocked by your father's sudden death.'

He meant well but Nancy escaped from his office as soon as she could. She didn't want to break down and cry in front of him.

She had assured Mr Plummer that she would be back but just at this moment she didn't really know if she would. After all, Britain was on the brink of war in this year of 1939. Some said it was inevitable, though Neville Chamberlain still proclaimed his high hopes of appeasement with Germany. Who knew what the future would bring.

She liked her job and the people she worked with. Not all large stores, she was sure, employed a nurse to tend to their employees' needs, but the work was varied and interesting, and because of the large furniture depository and the removals business connected with the store, there wasn't a shortage of patients for her to tend, with their trapped fingers, damaged toes where heavy furniture had landed, even the odd sprained wrist or ankle.

The train was pulling into yet another station. Nancy wiped the tears from her eyes and watched the other passengers alight. She seemed to have been on the train for hours and there was still some distance to go before they reached York. Many of the passengers were servicemen, some women too, in their neat uniforms, and seeing them the idea of a coming conflict was brought even nearer. Had call up started even now, Nancy wondered?

'Do you mind if I sit here?'

Nancy looked up to see that the rest of the travellers in her particular compartment had now left the train and a soldier was asking if he might join her? She found the polite request, quaint and touching, after all, this wasn't a *Ladies Only* compartment.

'Please do,' she said with a smile.

She expected others to join them but soon the train started to move off and no-one did. Perhaps there was now more room all along the train.

'Thank you,' the soldier said.

He took the window seat opposite her, after depositing his kit bag on the luggage rack, from which he had extracted a folded newspaper.

She glanced surreptitiously at him. He was quite young, with stripes on the sleeve of his jacket which she believed made him the rank of a sergeant. After a moment or two, he removed his cap and revealed short brown hair. He unfolded his newspaper and started to read it.

Nancy went back to looking out of the window, very much aware that each turn of the wheels was taking her back home.

Home! She had never thought of Kingston-on-Thames as home, not really, thought she had been happy there. When she wasn't working she lived a quiet, self-contained life, not often socialising. She had gone south on what was no more than a whim, and she knew that her father had been saddened by her decision to leave home, but he hadn't known, because she had never told him, the real reason she had to get out of Hepplestone.

An affair of the heart, she thought with a secret sigh, hence her desire for a sheltered life with no complications. Well, she was truly over her feelings for Dr Alec Bentley and had no qualms that he might be in Hepplestone. Her father had told her in one of his frequent letters, writing conversationally, having no idea what she and Alec had meant to each other, that he had taken on a practice in the Midlands and was a very busy man.

'I don't know why I bother to read the papers.' The soldier's voice startled her. She glanced at him, he was smiling and she noticed how his brown eyes crinkled at the corners when he did, giving him a boyish look.

'Doom and gloom I suppose,' Nancy remarked.

The soldier put the newspaper on the seat beside him. 'All the time,' he said.

'Have you been called up?' Nancy asked, feeling she must make some comment.

'No, I'm a regular soldier. I'm joining my regiment at Catterick Barracks. That's near York,' he added.

Nancy smiled. 'That's where I leave the train, too,' she said.

'You live in York?'

'No. In a small town near there. I'm . . . ' she hesitated then went on,

'I'm going home for my father's funeral.'

'Oh, I'm so sorry to hear that.' He looked sorry too and the expression of sympathy on his face was too much for Nancy.

To her horror she started to cry, fumbling in her bag for a hankie and seeming unable to find one. Immediately the soldier came to sit beside her, handing her a pristine white handkerchief of his own.

'Thank you,' Nancy murmured, dabbing at her eyes.

She then crushed the hankie in her fingers, not knowing quite what to do with it. She could hardly say, 'I'll launder it and let you have it back,' when she would never see him again.

Gently he removed the handkerchief from her fingers, putting it back in his pocket.

'Don't worry about it,' he said softly.

She was disappointed when he returned to his own side of the compartment. Somehow, she had felt his presence comforting.

'My name is Wallace, James Wallace,' he said next and leaned across to offer her his hand.

'Nancy Mellor,' she said, shaking hands. His grip was firm and strong.

He stared at her with a strange expression on his face. 'Nancy . . . '

His eyes had clouded over and he picked up his newspaper and opened it again, looking intently at what was written there.

Why had he said her name like that? With a kind of sadness in his voice. Just the one word, but it had seemed to say so much. He didn't seem inclined to make any further conversation and Nancy sat back in her seat and closed her eyes.

Surely the journey couldn't take much longer.

When she opened her eyes again she saw that the soldier had taken out a pen and a piece of paper and was writing something. She watched his bent head as his pen seemed to hover over the paper. Then he screwed the paper up and put it in the pocket of his tunic.

Nancy tried not to be too obvious but she was fascinated when James Wallace repeated his action a couple of more times. Writing quickly and briefly, pausing, even chewing the end of his expensive looking fountain pen then screwing up the paper again, with a jerky movement, as though he was angry with himself for not being able to complete whatever he was trying to write.

When he suddenly looked across at her, Nancy turned her head towards the window. She could see York Minster in the distance.

'We're nearly there,' she said.

She heard the soldier moving, reaching up to get his kit bag, turning to her to say, 'Shall I get your case, Miss Mellor?'

'Thank you.' Nancy pulled on her white gloves.

He put the case on the seat beside her. His smile had returned, the worried look had gone.

'I hope all goes well for you,' he said.

'And you.'

Once more he held out his hand and once again Nancy took it. 'Goodbye, Sergeant Wallace,' she said.

'Goodbye, Miss Mellor . . . Nancy,' he added rather shyly.

Then he was gone and Nancy gathered together her handbag and a paperback book which she hadn't even bothered to open.

As she started to leave the compartment she saw that the soldier had left his folded newspaper on his seat. She picked it up, looking out of the window, wondering if she would be able to catch his attention, but she could see him, striding along the crowded platform, tall and straight, his kit bag hoisted on to his shoulder.

He must have moved with the speed of light to be off the train so quickly. She decided she would leave the newspaper as some other passenger might like to read it when she saw a piece of paper flutter on to the floor. Out of curiosity she picked it up.

There were just three words written on it in scrawling blue ink.

My Dearest Nancy.

The soldier had not crumpled this sheet, but simply folded it in half as though intending to write more later. Nancy stared at the words, reading her own name. Who was this other Nancy? A wife? A sweetheart, perhaps?

Whoever she was, it had been obvious that Sergeant Wallace had not found the writing of what must surely be a letter an easy matter.

She refolded the piece of paper, unwilling, for some reason to throw it away. Carefully she slipped it into the pocket of her jacket.

It was to be some time later, after the funeral, before she remembered it was there.

2

Alfred Taylor was waiting outside York station with his taxi. He was a small, wiry man, always smiling, cheerful and helpful, but today his narrow face was solemn as he leapt forward to take Nancy's suitcase.

'Miss Mellor,' he greeted.

'Hello, Mr Taylor,' Nancy said, smiling at him. 'Thank you for meeting me.'

'My pleasure,' he said. 'I'll have you home in a jiffy.' He held on to her arm and guided her gently to the waiting taxi.

As soon as she was seated, Alfred turned in the driving seat to look at her.

'I'm that sorry about your father, Miss Mellor. It was a terrible shock. Well, it must have been to you too, of course. Such a wonderful man and one we can ill afford to lose. Especially now.' He shook his head sadly. 'God forbid it should come to a fight, but I, for one, shan't be holding me breath. 'Course, I'm too old for call up, more's the pity. Did my stint in the last war, but I'd like to have a crack at them Jerries all the same.'

Nancy let him chatter on, staring silently out of the windows as the taxi left York behind and took to the open road, familiar scenery flashing past the windows.

For a brief moment her mind dwelt on the young soldier, wondering in which direction he had travelled since he left the train. Had he, too, been met?

In no time at all it seemed they had reached the little market town of Hepplestone, where Dr Mellor had been a doctor since before Nancy was born. Her eyes were drawn to his surgery in the high street, shutters closed over its windows now as though the very building mourned the loss of such a good man.

What would have happened to all her

father's patients? There was another doctor, a Dr Farnsworth, in the next town, but he must be getting on in years now and surely close to retirement. Probably the services of a new doctor had been acquired, or a locum perhaps.

Alfred drove through the town and out on to a narrow country lane.

'Nearly there, Miss Mellor,' he called to her. 'I expect Mrs Hedges will be waiting for you. Ready with a nice cup of tea, no doubt.' He turned to grin at her.

No doubt. A nice cup of tea was her father's housekeeper's cure for all ills. There would be tears as well, Nancy was sure and knew she would have to steel herself not to give in to any of her own.

She was already thinking ahead to the funeral. The arrangements that must be made. People to notify, an advertisement in the local paper, that would be essential. And Aunt Helen to telephone, which would be the hardest thing of all to do. She lived in the Lake District and they didn't meet often, but she was John Mellor's only sister and would be heartbroken when she heard the news.

Suddenly, there was Poplar House in front of her, built of grey stone, solid and dependable looking with curtains drawn respectfully at all the windows. Thanks goodness, Nancy thought, that the sun was shining brightly. She couldn't bear glooms and shadows. Immediately she felt ashamed of her thoughts. Of course, dear Mrs Hedges would keep the rooms darkened; that was her way. She had worked for Dr Mellor for many years and would miss him as dreadfully as anyone.

Alfred opened the taxi door. 'Here we are. Safe and sound!' He was trying to be cheerful.

Nancy took out her purse and paid him, giving him a generous tip. He touched his cap.

'Thank you, miss,' he said. 'Shall I take your case inside for you?'

'No, thank you. I can manage.'

'Well, best be off. I seem to be rushed off me feet these days.' He climbed back into the driving seat and Nancy watched him go down the long drive and disappear from sight.

She turned and faced the house, drawing a deep breath.

'I'd better ring the bell,' she thought, though she had her own key.

She mounted the three semi-circular steps and lifted her hand, composing herself for what she felt sure would be an emotional meeting.

Aunt Helen said she would come at once, on the first available train. Despite her obvious shock her voice was calm and Nancy was glad she would soon be on her way. She had always felt close to her spinster aunt who had once, not too long ago, been a matron in a busy hospital, but was now retired and, in her own words 'doing what she wanted'; walking, painting, meeting her many friends. She had bought a large, lakeside house and

Nancy knew she loved living in the Lake District.

Nancy had wasted no time in sitting down and writing as many letters as she could think of, to friends and former colleagues of her father, making various telephone calls too. It was good to keep busy and she managed to remain so, at least during the day. But her first evening home was a different matter. After Mrs Hedges had retired to her own private sitting-room, Nancy sat in her father's favourite chair and looked out over the garden, not drawing the curtains until the shadows had lengthened and it was too dark to see.

During the day, in deference to Mrs Hedges, the curtains had been left in place, but Nancy couldn't bear to be enclosed when she was alone and staring at the long, smooth green lawns, kept in tip top condition by a local elderly gardening enthusiast, seemed to bring her comfort of a sort.

In bed, though, on that first night, she found it impossible to sleep and yearned for the moment her aunt would arrive. Dear Mrs Hedges was a treasure, but too fussy, too obliging and inclined to burst into tears at any given moment, covering her face with her apron and sobbing about 'Poor, dear, Dr Mellor.'

Of course, Nancy knew that Mrs Hedges had been the one to find her father, collapsed in his study and that must have been terrible for her, but she really did not want to be told over and over again just how terrible it had been.

It was on her second evening home when she was wearily thumbing through the depressing leaflets left by the funeral director that someone rang the door-bell.

Aunt Helen, of course, she thought and rushed to open the door, not wanting to disturb Mrs Hedges who would be listening to the wireless and doing her endless crocheting, but it wasn't her aunt. It was a tall, broad-shouldered young man with thick, sandy hair and vivid blue eyes.

He was wearing a dark suit, a sombre tie and he immediately leaned forward and kissed Nancy lightly on the cheek.

'Nancy; I'm so sorry. I had to come.'

'Alec,' she said, knowing she must ask him in and not wanting to, but opening the door for him anyway.

'How did you know?' she asked, feeling guilty because she had not sent Dr Bentley a letter to tell him of her father's death. On the other hand, she would have had to make a conscious effort to obtain his present address and had preferred to push thoughts of him to the back of her mind.

But he was here now and as they walked into the sitting-room he said, 'There was an announcement in The Lancet.'

This surprised Nancy, it hadn't been placed by her. It just went to show how fast news travelled, good or bad.

Alec took hold of her hand and she let it lie there. 'Oh, Nancy, I don't know what to say. It was only a couple of weeks ago that I heard from John . . . '

Sharply Nancy interrupted, 'You kept in regular touch?'

Alec nodded, sitting down on the sofa, hitching up his immaculately creased trousers. 'Oh, yes.' He smiled. He had a very boyish face but one that Nancy knew from past experience, could become sullen and poutish. 'John told me all about what you were doing, you know.'

Did he now, she thought.

Aloud she said, 'I expect you'd like a drink.' She half rose out of her seat.

'No, don't bother. I shan't stay long, I know you must have a great deal on your mind. But I just had to be here for you.'

Nancy winced. She didn't want him here for her. She didn't want him here at all. When they had parted over three years ago, she had hoped that was the last she would see of him.

'Where are you staying?' she asked him, sitting down again.

'In Hepplestone. The Red Lion. I arrived earlier today. Just for the funeral, of course, then I'll be going back.'

She felt she should ask, 'Back to where?' but she didn't. She knew he would tell her anyway.

'My practice has doubled in the last three years, but now, of course, I'm faced with something of a dilemma, I'm afraid.'

'In what way?' Nancy hoped Mrs Hedges would come in, but in the next instant she decided that would be disastrous.

There would be a tearful display, lots of hugs and kisses and worst of all, an offer for Alec to stay with them. The young, dashing doctor had always been a favourite of Mrs Hedges ever since he came to act as Dr Mellor's assistant. Well, he hadn't stayed long, much too ambitious to only be second-in-command so to speak and, then there'd been their spectacular break-up when she discovered he was seeing someone else behind her back.

But that was all in the past. All

Nancy need be concerned about now was being polite to her guest, and humbly accepting his no doubt genuine condolences.

Alec looked down and studied his well kept finger nails.

'Did you know, Nancy, that your father was considering retiring?'

She was shocked. No, she hadn't known that. He had said nothing to her.

Alec didn't wait for her to reply. He went on, 'It seems his health wasn't too good. Oh, I never had the slightest idea he would die so suddenly, but I did know he wasn't as well as he should be.' He looked at her stricken face. 'I'm sorry, Nancy, I can see he hadn't told you.'

She felt angry that her father had found fit to confide in Alec but not in her, but then she realised it was typical of him. He wouldn't have wanted her to worry about him. Tears filled her eyes, but she fought them back, she would not cry in front of Alec.

Alec was talking quickly now, as

though he needed to get something off his chest. 'He offered me his practice and I must say I was very tempted. I love it round here; the Midlands doesn't compare with Yorkshire any day of the week.'

Nancy couldn't believe what she was hearing, but again, Alec gave her no chance to speak.

'I told John I would give it serious thought, but then, this happened and now I don't really know what to do. If I jump straight into John's shoes it might look bad. On the other hand . . . '

At last his words dried up.

'Well,' Nancy spoke in a quiet, prim voice, 'you must do as you see fit, Alec,' wondering how it would leave her if Alec did move back to Yorkshire and take up the surgery in the high street.

Only now did she admit to herself that she, too, had been considering moving back home. With her qualifications she would surely be able to get work up here and she had long toyed with the idea of gaining even further qualifications and skills. She knew that Leeds General Infirmary was a teaching hospital, perhaps she could be taken on there, it wasn't far away, then she could live here.

But now . . . now, Alec had ruined all that by his shock announcement. Of course he would step into John's shoes. He would be in sole charge of the practice and should Dr Farnsworth retire in the near future, that surgery would be up for grabs as well.

There was an awkward silence between them. Even Alec seemed to have lost his voice. He was looking at her intently and she wondered whether he expected her to congratulate him, tell him how pleased she was, but she wasn't because Hepplestone wasn't big enough for the both of them.

The shrill sound of the doorbell startled her. She jumped up, 'That will be Aunt Helen,' she cried, praying that she was right this time.

She hurried from the room just as

Mrs Hedges appeared from the back of the house.

'Two visitors in one day, Miss Nancy,' she cried, 'more flowers, more condolences I expect.'

'I'll see to it, Mrs Hedges,' Nancy said kindly, hoping the housekeeper wouldn't peer into the sitting-room. At least not just yet.

She wouldn't be able to keep Alec Bentley a secret for long. She had no hopes of that.

3

Nancy stood before the long mirror in her bedroom. Black had never been her colour, she decided, but she could hardly wear anything different. The dress she had chosen was startlingly plain, with tiny pearl buttons at the neck and cuffs. She had put up her long, dark hair, twisting it into a pleat at the back of her head.

Her face was pale, her eyes two dark pools. Over the intervening days since she returned to Hepplestone, she had managed to come to terms with her father's death, but now was the final ordeal; to see her father laid to rest in the small churchyard, close to her mother's grave.

She knew that the church would be filled with mourners, for Dr John Mellor had been a much loved and well respected figure in the area, building up the trust and admiration of his patients over the years. A friend more than a family doctor.

He would be sadly missed.

Many of the mourners would be returning to the house after the service to partake of the refreshments lovingly prepared by Mrs Hedges who, this morning had decided to put a brave face on things and was doing what she loved best, supervising the preparation of the sandwiches, cakes and drinks in her well-equipped kitchen. She had enlisted the help of her good friend, Rose, who lived on the edge of the town.

Someone tapped on the bedroom door and Nancy called out, 'Come in,' sure it would be her Aunt Helen.

It was. She, too, was wearing black but her smart, two piece costume was relieved somewhat by a crisp white collar. She was a good-looking woman in her early fifties, John Mellor's only sister.

'How are you feeling, dear?' she

asked with a smile.

'I'm all right,' Nancy said.

That didn't really sum up how she felt. She picked up the small close-fitting hat and her black gloves from the bed.

Helen came further into the room. 'We'd better go downstairs, Nancy,' she said quietly.

Nancy took a deep breath, following her aunt out of the room. Mrs Hedges, and Rose, who were both coming to the funeral, were standing in the hall, sombrely dressed as Nancy was sure everybody would be on this solemn occasion. Mrs Hedges moved forward and touched Nancy's arm.

'Keep your chin up, Miss Nancy,' she said, but her own considerable chin was quivering. 'Rose and me have got everything ready.'

'Yes, thank you, Mrs Hedges,' Nancy murmured.

She realised that Mrs Hedges was now the one supporting her, rather than the other way round.

The scent of flowers in the church was almost over-powering. Nancy saw Alec Bentley almost at once. He wasn't yet seated, but standing inside the porch, as though waiting for her to arrive. He gave her a warm smile, but she merely nodded her head in acknowledgement.

The service began, with some of Dr Mellor's favourite hymns and an address from Dr Farnsworth, who had called to see Nancy earlier and had asked if he might have the honour of saying a few words. Nancy had been happy to let him.

He looked well, though silver-haired and slightly stooped now; still practising, of course. Nancy felt a little stab of pain when she thought how her own father had lost his life while in his prime.

She gave herself over to the service and later everyone emerged into the late morning sunshine to witness the interment of the good doctor.

Then it was back to the house where

Mrs Hedges and Rose, without removing their hats, donned crisp white aprons and took over the responsibility of hostesses, for which Nancy was grateful. This gave her the opportunity of sitting quietly, receiving people's kind remarks, some handshakes, some kisses.

There was a vase of late summer roses on the sitting room windowsill and Nancy breathed in the almost cloying perfume, recalling vividly the scent of the flowers in the church. Tears were very near at that moment, but she managed a tremulous smile when Aunt Helen came over to her.

'You haven't got a drink, Nancy,' Aunt Helen said, 'Shall I get you one?'

Nancy shook her head. 'No, thank you. I'll have some tea later, when everyone's left.'

'Are you sure, dear?' Her aunt looked worried.

'Perfectly. Ah, here comes Alec. I was wondering how long it would be before he sought me out.'

Aunt Helen had been introduced to

Dr Bentley the day she arrived at the house, but all she knew of him was that he was a doctor-friend of her brother's. She moved away now, as Alec came over to where Nancy was sitting, bending low over her chair and speaking in a quiet voice.

'Let's go out into the garden, Nancy,' he suggested.

She wasn't so sure she wanted to do that, it would be nice to get some fresh air, but with Alec . . . ? He was already drawing her to her feet so she didn't have much choice.

'Have you come to a decision yet, Alec?' Nancy asked him as they started to walk along the crazy paving terrace in front of the house.

'Yes. I shall be moving to Hepplestone as soon as I can settle my affairs.'

'Congratulations.'

He acknowledged her words with a slight bow. 'Thank you. I hope we will be able to remain friends, Nancy. We shall probably be seeing a great deal of one another.'

Not if she could help it. Her mind was dwelling on her earlier idea of getting in touch with the Leeds General Infirmary to see if they could offer her a place there. If she was lucky, she would be living in for most of the time, but would still keep Poplar House open. She couldn't stop Alec taking up his new position, but being his friend was not what she wanted.

However, this was not the time or the place to tell him so and she wisely said nothing. She was relieved when she saw Aunt Helen coming across the grass towards her.

'Some of the guests are leaving, Nancy,' she said.

'I'll come at once.' Nancy was glad to hurry away from Alec who stood watching the two women walk away with a perplexed look on his face.

The perceptive older woman quickly picked up on Nancy's relief at being rescued.

'Was he bothering you, Nancy?' she asked.

Nancy laughed. 'Bothering me? Alec? Oh, no. I'll tell you all about it some time, Aunt Helen.'

It was later in the day when Aunt Helen joined Nancy in the sitting room. The house was quiet again, neat and tidy and all the cars had gone from the drive. Mrs Hedges and her friend had dealt with the mountains of washing up and were sitting in the housekeeper's sitting room, with their feet up presumably, having a natter and finishing off the remains of the sherry.

'I've been wanting to talk to you, Nancy,' Aunt Helen began. She sat in the chair opposite her niece's. 'Perhaps this isn't the right time, but you know I have to leave in the morning so I didn't want to lose the opportunity.'

Nancy felt curious. 'What is it?' she said.

'I wondered if you'd thought about what you were going to do now.'

'Well, I could go back to Kingston-on-Thames, of course . . .'

Helen frowned. 'Is that wise, in view

33

of the present situation?'

'We're not at war yet, Aunt Helen,' Nancy said, 'and Kingston is a few miles from London. I'm sure I would be all right, but I'm not all that certain it's what I want to do. I have a need, I think, to spend more time here, where Dad and I . . . ' she broke off as tears, as so often happened lately, threatened.

'That's only natural, dear,' Aunt Helen said.

'I have to consider Mrs Hedges too. If I closed up the house, or sold it, what would she do?'

'Hasn't Mrs Hedges mentioned her plans to you?' Aunt Helen asked.

'What plans?' Nancy stared at her.

'Oh, dear, have I spoken out of turn? It's just that I accidentally overheard Mrs Hedges talking to her friend, Rose, saying something about retiring and moving in with her sister. She said that now that John had 'passed over' as she put it, it might be time she hung up her apron.' Helen smiled. 'My words, not hers, of course.'

'She's not mentioned it to me,' Nancy confessed.

'Then I'm sorry I mentioned it, dear.'

'No, no, that's all right. I'm glad I know. It makes things easier for me. Of course, I shall wait till Mrs Hedges broaches the subject herself, but if she really does want to retire, that will be one load off my mind.' She paused and smoothed out an imaginary crease in her skirt. 'There's another option I'm considering, too. I thought I might contact the Leeds General Infirmary to see if I can get a place there. It's a teaching hospital, you know.'

Helen smiled. 'Yes, I did know that,' she said.

'Of course,' Nancy smiled too. 'I was forgetting. Anyway, doing that is uppermost in my mind at the moment.'

'Well, that makes what I have to ask you so much easier, Nancy,' Helen went on.

'Oh?' Nancy's interest quickened.

'You might not know it, but I've been regretting my departure from the medical profession of late, and because of the threat of war, I, too, have come to a decision. I've been in touch with the powers that be, so to speak, and I've decided to turn Greystones into a convalescent home for war casualties.'

Nancy frowned. 'Isn't that a little premature?' she asked.

'I don't think so, Nancy. Make no mistake about it, war is inevitable. Do you really think that Hitler is going to stop without being made to? He's in Poland now, remember.'

Nancy could hear the urgency, the suppressed anger in her aunt's voice. She felt somewhat ashamed that, though she had read about the possibility of war, and heard all the news on the wireless, she hadn't really dwelt on it. There had been so much else to occupy her thoughts.

Now she said, 'It's a wonderful idea.'

'Well, as they say, 'Your country needs you' and that's where you come in, Nancy.'

'Me? How?'

'I want you to come in with me. Don't give me your decision now, everything's still in the planning stage, of course, but, don't you see, if you do enroll at the LGI for a year or so, then come to me I shall certainly be able to use you, and your skills.'

Nancy's smile was ironic. 'So you think the war, once it starts, will drag on?'

'I remember the Great War too well, Nancy,' Helen said with a touch of the same irony.

It was a great deal for Nancy to take in, but her aunt assured her that it didn't have to be an overnight decision. Plenty of time to follow her own dreams, and the more she thought about it, the more Nancy realised that this was a way forward for her. A new beginning.

She would have to let Mr Plummer know of her decision, of course, and she didn't think he would be too happy to lose her. On the other hand, he was a very patriotic man and would, Nancy felt certain, thoroughly approve of what Aunt Helen was going to do.

'Of course, I have to tell myself that the Leeds General might not want me,' she said now.

'Negative thinking,' Aunt Helen said with a frown. 'Oh, we can't have that, can we?'

Dr Mellor's will had been read the afternoon of his funeral. Its content came as no surprise to Nancy, but as quite a surprise to some people, including Mrs Hedges and various good people of Hepplestone.

After Helen had left the next morning, the house seemed empty again and loneliness settled on Nancy. The weather was changing too, a definite chill in the air, especially as evening drew on. September was nearly here and soon summer would be over for another year.

To occupy her time, Nancy decided to pack away some of her summer clothes. She had always kept a wardrobe of clothes at Poplar House, plus the ones she had brought with her. Now would be the time to arrange for the rest of her things to be forwarded on to her.

She had a good friend and neighbour, with whom she had left a key and knew when the time came this friend would be more than happy to do the packing and despatching for her. The flat she rented was furnished, so it was only a matter of certain personal effects and clothing.

Making this decision made Nancy realise that she had now fully made up her mind. She would not be returning to Kingston.

Her light linen jacket and straw hat with the small bunch of pink roses on it in which she had travelled home, was still hanging in the hall where she had left it and she gathered them up to take them upstairs. It was as she folded the jacket over her arm that she remembered the piece of paper she had slipped into the pocket that day on the train.

Sergeant James Wallace sprang immediately to her mind. Her fingers closed over the folded paper and she took it out and read again what was written there.

My Dearest Nancy . . .

She hoped James and his Nancy had made up their differences and that he was safe and well.

As the noise of approaching war rumbled on, the wireless seemed to be about nothing else, James Wallace and his fellow soldiers must be in a state of constant alertness, for their lives would change irrevocably once the hostilities began.

Nancy went upstairs, still holding the piece of paper in her hand. She knew she would be unable to throw it away, and she put it in the back of her mother-of-pearl backed Bible, given to her by her father on her Confirmation Day. Nancy wasn't particularly religious, but nevertheless always kept the Bible on her bedside table.

Now she kept her hand on the bible

for several seconds as though reluctant to walk away, as though she needed to hold on to it, not only to remember her beloved father, but also the young soldier who had so impressed her.

She only moved when there came a rap on the bedroom door.

It was Mrs Hedges standing there, an anxious-faced Mrs Hedges and Nancy knew why she was there.

4

'I need to have a word with you if I may, Miss Nancy,' the rather nervous housekeeper began.

'Of course, Mrs Hedges. Shall we go downstairs?' She had long since given up hope of Mrs Hedges dropping the 'Miss' when addressing her. When she was a child she had always been plain 'Nancy' but somewhere around her sixteenth birthday she had become 'Miss Nancy' and now she was stuck with it.

'No, I can tell you here,' Mrs Hedges went on.

Nancy could see she was nervous and on edge so she said gently, leading the older woman to a basket chair where she sat down, apparently with some relief, 'Is it about your retirement, Mrs Hedges?'

The housekeeper shot her a surprised

glance. 'How did you know?'

Nancy smiled. 'Let's say a little bird told me.' Then as Mrs Hedges was about to protest, 'No, not Rose, she hadn't said a word. It was Aunt Helen, actually, she overheard your conversation.'

The worried look increased on Mrs Hedge's face. 'Oh, I don't know what to say,' she murmured.

Nancy sat on the edge of the bed. 'You've been a good friend both to Dad and me, Mrs Hedges,' she said, 'you've been here some years, haven't you?'

'Oh, yes, a long, long time and I've loved every minute of it. But now that dear Dr Mellor has gone . . . ' her voice trailed off and she wiped her eyes on a corner of her apron.

Nancy leaned forward and patted her plump fingers. 'You feel you need a change and a rest, too, of course. I understand fully.'

'Then you won't mind me handing in my notice, so to speak.'

'Not at all. Actually, I don't really

know what I shall be doing myself in the future, even if I'll want to keep Poplar House on, so it suits us both, doesn't it?'

She asked where Mrs Hedges was going, pretending she hadn't heard that bit from Aunt Helen, and then listened to Mrs Hedges going on at some length about her sister, Doris, and her little bungalow and that they both had a bit put by, and dear Dr Mellor had been so generous to her in his will and it was only the other side of York she was moving to, and so on and so forth, but when Mrs Hedges finally went back to her kitchen, Nancy could see she was happy and content and, yes, quite excited about the future.

As I must be, she thought.

Nancy was surprised to find Alec Bentley on her doorstep a couple of days later. More casually dressed than at the funeral, with a dark sweater over a pale blue shirt.

'I thought you'd gone back to the Midlands,' she said.

'I was going to, but I couldn't leave without seeing you, Nancy.'

She felt a quick surge of anger which she managed to suppress. He was beginning to be a nuisance. Thank goodness there was now a strong possibility that the Leeds General would take her on. She was going there the next afternoon. She could not wait to tell Alec this.

Reluctantly she invited him in. Mrs Hedges was at Rose's so there would be no gushing offers of tea and biscuits and it was certainly not Nancy's intention to offer either.

Alec settled himself, uninvited, in an armchair.

'I felt you were trying to avoid me at the funeral,' he said.

'Did you?' she remarked cagily, deciding that although Alec was seated she would remain standing.

'Your aunt seemed to provide a very proficient chaperone.'

Nancy made no remark to that and Alec went on, 'This is silly, Nancy. I'm

45

taking over your father's practice so it's inevitable we shall see a great deal of one another.'

'Not necessarily,' Nancy told him smugly and went on to tell him about her interview in Leeds.

He seemed surprised. 'That's very sudden, isn't it?'

'No. I've been thinking about it for some time. If a war is coming, I don't want necessarily to be so close to the capital. And I have to earn my living, Alec, just like everybody else.'

Alec stood up then and moved towards her. 'If you married me, Nancy, you wouldn't need to earn a living. I would be more than capable of providing for you.'

She almost laughed at that. Almost, but not quite. It was too outrageous for laughter.

'Have you forgotten we were going out with one another for over two years. Marriage had been mentioned then, as I recall, but that didn't stop you deceiving me with Lucy Patterson.'

She was glad Alec had the grace to blush. 'That was a mistake and if I may say so, you over-reacted going away as you did, calling the whole thing off.'

She did show her anger then, 'Stop it, Alec!' she yelled. 'Please understand that I don't love you any more. Perhaps I never did love you.' As she said those words, she realised they were true. She had never loved Alec Bentley. Only her pride had been hurt when he played around. Perhaps she had over-reacted in her decision to leave Hepplestone, but only in that.

'I can't believe that, Nancy.' He looked like a scolded schoolboy, but when he tried to take her in his arms she moved quickly away from him.

'As you say, our meeting in the future will probably be inevitable,' she said, 'but I'm hoping to be working at the Leeds General Infirmary before long, and I hope you will respect my privacy as I intend to respect yours. Now, will you please leave. I'm rather busy.' She wasn't.

'May I drive you to Leeds?' Alec asked plaintively.

'No, thank you, I have Dad's car. Are you forgetting I learned to drive when I was nineteen?'

He gave a sort of rueful grin. 'So you did. Well, I suppose I must wish you luck. See you around!' And he turned on his heels and left her so abruptly she felt almost stunned.

Then when she heard the front door closing rather loudly she relaxed.

On the day Nancy commenced her duties at the Leeds General, war was finally declared.

Neville Chamberlain broadcast to the nation, in a sad and sombre voice, that Hitler had refused to withdraw his troops from Poland and that, consequently, this country was at war with Germany.

So it had finally happened and now nothing would ever be the same again.

From the window of her bedroom, over the tree tops, Nancy could see the dull waters of Windermere. In the summer she could imagine the sun glinting on the water, the trees in full leaf and yachts and other craft gliding over the lake. Now, in the middle of October 1941, and on a dull day the sight was more sombre.

It was difficult to comprehend that the war was now starting its third year. The optimists had been wrong, the doom and gloom prophets right, this war was destined to drag on and on.

So much had changed in Nancy's life. To her surprise she and Alec had managed to become friends, he had not tried to push her into a direction she did not wish to go. When they met and it wasn't as often as she had thought it would be, they were at first merely civil to one another, but then, when Nancy no longer felt threatened, and realised he wasn't such a bad sort after all.

He took over the practice and when Nancy finally left the Leeds General he was in negotiation with Dr Farnsworth to take on his practice as well.

He had wished her well in her new

venture. 'You'll go far, Nancy,' he told her, kissing her lightly on the cheek. 'Your aunt is a very lucky woman to have you at her side.'

Nancy was pleased by his words but was a little worried because he seemed distant somehow; pre-occupied.

'Is anything wrong, Alec?' she asked.

They had gone for one of their rare meals out in York. The menu was wartime fare, stolid and unvarying and the restaurant was dimly lit, but Nancy enjoyed the occasions; Alec could be quite amusing when he tried.

'I suppose it's the war that's getting to me,' Alec said, fiddling with his fork. 'I know I'm doing a worthwhile job but I feel I should be doing more.'

'Joining up, you mean?'

'Well, yes.'

'But you're in a reserved occupation,' Nancy reminded him, 'the people of Hepplestone, and Norland too, of course, need you.'

'I suppose so,' Alec reluctantly agreed.

But he wasn't his usual, cheerful self.

Then, within the week, Nancy was on her way to join Aunt Helen at Greystones and Alec became the furthest thing from her mind.

She turned when someone tapped on the door. Aunt Helen put her head round, a very different looking Aunt Helen from the one who had come to John Mellor's funeral. Now she wore the uniform of a hospital matron, starched and crisp, her hair severely pulled back under her cap. But her face still held the same kind, gentle expression.

Nancy, too, was wearing her uniform.

'Should I address you as Matron, Aunt Helen?' she asked.

'On the wards, yes, I suppose you must, but in private, I'm still your Aunt Helen.' She walked towards the window where Nancy was still standing. 'Lovely view, isn't it?'

'It is.'

'I am sure it has a calming effect on young men. I can't bring myself to think of them as patients, though, of course, that's what they are.'

Nancy recalled her visit to the wards the previous evening, soon after her arrival at the large stone house with its neat gardens and lake view. She remembered the house well from her previous visits, but now it had been transformed. Some of the once grand reception rooms were now wards where servicemen of all ranks and ages recovered from their injuries. Some, Nancy knew, would never go back to active duty; others would be patched up and returned to the front.

Aunt Helen had enlisted a small but efficient staff and Nancy felt proud to be among them.

'You've done really well, Nancy,' Aunt Helen said. 'Completing your extended training so quickly.'

Nancy smiled. 'Perhaps it's because there's a war on,' she said, 'and as many nurses as possible are needed.'

Helen put her hand on Nancy's shoulder. 'Don't run yourself down, dear,' she advised, 'I have every faith in you. Are you ready to meet your charges?' She gave a mischievous smile. 'I know you met some of them last night, but most of them were asleep. This morning they'll be bright and chirpy, ready for their breakfasts. As it's such a cold, dull morning I doubt many of them will want to venture out, but if the sun comes out, however chill the air, I shall expect to see the boys taking exercise, or being wheeled down to the lake in their chairs.'

Nancy took a deep breath. 'I'm ready,' she said.

'We have a new young man arriving today,' Helen went on. 'A Captain in the Royal Artillery. He's had a bad leg wound, though it seems to be healing well, so I'm told. The main problem is his eyes . . . it's early days yet and we live in hope, but his eyes are bandaged at the moment. I haven't met him yet, of course, but I've been advised that he is also . . . emotionally damaged.'

Nancy's heart went out to his young

captain. 'Shell shocked?' she asked.

Helen shook her head. 'No, nothing like that. It's his private and personal life that is the cause. I haven't been told much about Captain Wallace, except to be forewarned that he might be difficult, morose and depressed.' She braced her shoulders. 'Well, we shall endeavour to look after him as best we can, won't we, Nancy?'

'Of course,' but Nancy wasn't really listening any more.

Captain Wallace. The name rang a bell. But she didn't know many servicemen, and those she did were from Hepplestone, and none, of whatever rank or regiment was called Wallace.

She shrugged the matter aside. Perhaps it would come to her later. There was a busy morning ahead. Bed baths to arrange, trays to be carried to bedsides, temperatures to take, sheets to change. Some of the occupants were walking about, some on crutches, other's with the aid of a stick; there was one soldier who had lost an arm, some were wearing their uniforms, others in pyjamas and dressing-gowns, yet others lying in bed, resting on high pillows, looking tired or listless or disorientated.

But on the other hand there was a cheerfulness about the place. Laughter, banter, even whistling or singing. Some wanted to tease the nurses, some to flirt, others to call for attention when it wasn't really necessary, but Nancy took it all in her stride and the day seemed to fly by.

She was having her lunch when the army ambulance arrived, bringing, she supposed, the young Royal Artillery Captain. She watched out of the window as a wheelchair was wheeled down the ramp.

She couldn't make out his face as both eyes were heavily bandaged. He was holding a walking stick in his right hand and when he got to the main entrance, where yet another ramp had been placed, he struggled to his feet. One of the orderlies reached for his arm but the Captain shrugged him off and limped unaided up the steps, stumbling when he reached the open doors. Only then when he didn't know which way to turn did he allow himself to be guided into the building.

Nancy finished her lunch and was leaving the dining hall when Aunt Helen came out of her office further along the corridor.

'Ah, Nurse Mellor,' she began, aware that there were other staff members and patients about. 'Captain Wallace has arrived. I'm putting him in room four at least for the time being, so he can be assessed.'

This room, Nancy knew was a single room. Personally she felt he might be better off among other men, he wouldn't have the same opportunities to brood, but it wasn't up to her.

'Would you like to assist me, nurse?'

'Yes, Matron, of course,' Nancy said.

They walked briskly along the long, smoothly floored corridor. All the walls were now painted pale green and white.

There were no pictures, only notices indicating the direction of the wards or the sun lounge or the library. The few single rooms were along the corridor on the other side of the entrance hall, ground floor rooms with views of both lake and garden.

Not that any of that would be of interest to Captain Wallace, Nancy thought sadly.

The orderlies had settled the young soldier in a chair by his neatly made bed. He was holding his stick firmly in both hands, his knuckles showing white as he gripped it.

'Good afternoon, Captain Wallace,' Aunt Helen greeted him cheerfully.

He turned his head swiftly in the direction of her voice. 'Good afternoon. Whom do I have the pleasure of addressing?' His voice was polite but cool.

'I am Matron and this is Nurse Mellor.'

'Hello,' Nancy spoke in little more than a whisper.

Now she was close to him, despite the bandages, she recognised him immediately. The shape of his face, his voice. She couldn't see his eyes, those friendly brown eyes that had crinkled at the corners when he smiled, but it was him. The soldier from the train. Now a Captain. Now wounded, blinded perhaps and very sad.

'How do you do, ladies?' he said with a forced cheerfulness that did not escape either of them.

There was no light of recognition in his voice. But why should there be, she had introduced herself as Nancy Mellor on that day in 1939, but that was over two years ago. So much had happened since then, to both of them.

5

The weather brightened the next day. The sun shone and the terrace in front of the house became a sun trap which encouraged some of the patients to sit outside or to stroll in the lovely gardens, if they were able to. In the distance the sun dappled the waters of Windermere. With the colours of autumn beginning to appear on the trees it was a beautiful sight.

Nancy knew she would not find Captain Wallace outdoors. He had not appeared outside his room since his arrival, though she knew he could walk about quite well with the aid of his stick. Her duties had kept her occupied elsewhere, but that morning she was determined to find out how he was faring so she asked Aunt Helen if she could take him his lunch.

Helen smiled. 'You've taken him

under your wing, haven't you?' she asked.

Nancy blushed. Was it so obvious? It was true she had enquired after his welfare several times.

'Don't be embarrassed, dear,' Helen went on, 'it's not unusual for a nurse to feel a certain rapport with a particular patient.'

'He seems so . . . sad,' Nancy said, 'oh, I know they've all been through so much, but Captain Wallace . . . ' she couldn't find the words to describe how she felt about him.

Aunt Helen nodded. 'He's already asked me if we've heard from his fiancée. Sadly, I had to tell him we hadn't, but I'm sure we will.'

Was this the other Nancy, the one Captain Wallace had had such difficulty writing to?

She considered telling her aunt that she had met Captain Wallace before, but decided against it.

When it was time for lunches to be served she took a tray to room 4.

Chicken soup and lightly buttered bread, well, margarine really, together with a small dish of raspberry jelly and a pouring of evaporated milk. Not much of a meal for a soldier, Nancy thought, but it was policy to give light nourishment in the first few days of assessment.

Captain Wallace was sitting in his chair, the stick held in both hands as before. As soon as Nancy opened the door he called out, 'Who is that?'

'Nurse Mellor,' she said, 'I've brought your lunch.'

'Ah, Nurse Mellor. You're the one who came in yesterday with your formidable Matron, aren't you?'

Nancy stiffened. 'Matron is not formidable, she's very kind.'

'Of course she is. And what delicacy have you brought me today, Nurse Mellor?' There was a slight sarcastic edge of his voice which Nancy decided to ignore.

'Chicken soup and raspberry jelly.' She moved and set the tray on a table near his chair.

'Not enough to get me back to fighting fit, is it?'

Which is precisely what she herself had been thinking.

'Do you need any help, Captain Wallace?' she asked, looking down at the top of his head. He still had the same cap of close-cropped brown hair. She stared at the back of his neck, how vulnerable it made him look, like a young boy.

But he wasn't a boy, he was a man; a soldier who had no doubt seen many terrible things.

'I do not!' he snapped suddenly. 'As you can see my arms and hands are fully usable. And I am old enough and steady enough to guide a soup spoon to my mouth, thank you.'

'In that case,' Nancy began, 'I'll leave you to it.'

She turned but suddenly he reached out and touched her hand. A soft, undemanding touch.

'I'm sorry, Nurse, that was very rude of me,' he said. 'But I can manage to feed myself, honestly I can.' He softened the words with the first smile Nancy had seen on him.

Except of course for the smiles which had crinkled his brown eyes on the train from Kings Cross.

He took a spoonful of soup; as he had said his hand was as steady as a rock which surprised her. Many soldiers when they first arrived, Aunt Helen had told her, were shaky and uncertain in their movements even when their injuries were less serious than Captain Wallace's.

'Very good,' he said, 'my compliments to the chef.'

Nancy couldn't be sure if every phrase he uttered wasn't one of sarcasm but she decided to give him the benefit of the doubt.

'Do you need anything else, Captain Wallace?' she asked.

'No, thank you. I have a bell close to my bed if I knock anything over.'

As she opened the door he called out, 'Nurse Mellor, any . . . messages for me? A letter, perhaps? A phone call?'

'I'm sorry, no,' Nancy said.

For a brief instant his hand holding the spoon was unsteady, rattling against the side of the soup bowl but he quickly regained his composure.

'Am I surprised?' he seemed to mutter the words to himself.

Nancy left, feeling a swift rise of irritation against the unknown Nancy, for she felt certain she was the one that James Wallace had become engaged to. If indeed they had not already been engaged when she met him on the train. She remembered the concentration on his face as he tried to compose that letter; the way he had crumpled the paper not once but twice and then, even on the third attempt being unable to write more than those three words, *My Dearest Nancy*.

She remembered also that she still had that piece of paper and felt guilty about that. It wasn't her property, she should have destroyed it as she had meant to do, but even knowing this she took it from her bible the moment she went back to her room.

The words told her more than they had the first time she had read them. But was this strictly true . . . ? This embittered young man was obviously waiting helplessly for word from his fiancée. Why hadn't she contacted him? She must know he had been brought here.

If she were Captain Wallace's fiancée she would have moved heaven and earth to contact him, and Aunt Helen had told her that the Captain was suffering from emotional stress associated with his private life. Didn't that knowledge in itself speak volumes?

Nancy put the paper away. She would never destroy it, she couldn't. It was a symbol of hope. They were engaged, promised to each other, that must mean something. She decided to reserve her judgement till she had met the other Nancy for herself.

Over the next few days, Nancy kept finding excuses to go to room 4. The

Captain's water jug needed replenishing; his bed needed straightening; the French windows needed opening to let in the fresh air as the milder, brighter weather continued. Anything and everything. She didn't neglect her regular duties on ward 7 upstairs, of course, she simply worked harder and faster.

There were six beds in ward 7, three of the occupants were at the moment bedfast, but all were cheerful and outgoing and no trouble at all to Nurse Mellor or anyone else. Indeed she looked forward to seeing them; their attitude would brighten up any day.

Two young sergeants occupied beds four and five. One was the man who had lost an arm and the other a red-headed Scot who wore his kilt with pride and was almost ready to be discharged, his wounds being serious in the first instance but mainly deep cuts and gashes to his face and chest from broken glass. His stitches had been removed and he would soon be rejoining his Scottish regiment. Something, Nancy knew, he could hardly wait for.

'Let me get at those Krauts,' she had heard him say more than once, as he brandished an imaginary weapon, a claymore perhaps she thought with a smile.

The sixth bed was still empty after the last occupant had been discharged. Nancy wondered whether Aunt Helen was considering putting Captain Wallace in this ward. Secretly she hoped not, though this thought caused her some guilt. She was sure the presence of other men would benefit him, help him to adjust as so many had done before him.

As it was he spent most of the day on his own and this couldn't be good for him. But she wanted an opportunity to help bring him out of himself.

His sadness sickened her, his veiled sarcasm upset her. She knew he needed time. At present none of them, not least Captain Wallace himself, knew what the outcome would be once his bandages had been removed. He was bound to be worried and on edge, and the continued silence from his fiancée was not helping in the least.

One morning she entered his room, after knocking loudly on the door. She always did this now as it made him aware that someone was coming in. She was surprised when the room was empty.

The sheets were thrown back and the Captain's dressing gown had gone from the edge of the bed but there was no sign of him.

Then she heard his voice. 'Is that you, Nurse Mellor? I'm out here, feeling the sun on my face.'

The French windows were wide open. Someone, perhaps the captain himself, had taken a chair out there and he was sitting with his head resting on the back, legs outstretched. For once his hands were relaxed and not clutching the ever present stick.

'How did you know it was me?' she asked.

'I can tell your knock. I can tell your footsteps. They're light. Matron walks heavily and she gives one single rap on the door. The nurse who brings my medicine always enters with a cheery greeting and the person who clears away my empty dishes has a persistent cough. I hope it isn't catching,' he finished with a grin.

He was very alert this morning. Nancy almost asked him if he had had a welcome letter, but thought better of it. If he hadn't he could well sink back into his usual morose state. She didn't want that to happen.

'Beautiful day, isn't it?' he said next.

'We're very lucky,' Nancy agreed, looking out over the garden. As the house was built on the top of a slight hill the views were quite spectacular.

It was strange talking to this young man whose eyes she could not see nor could she gauge his reactions.

His eyes had been one of the first things she had noticed about him on the train that day.

His head turned away again. Then he said, 'Just listen, nurse, isn't that wonderful?'

She listened but could hardly hear a sound. Leaves rustling in the light breeze, somewhere at the other end of the garden a burst of laughter, but very little else, not out here away from the always present sounds of the house.

He noticed her hesitation.

'The silence,' he said, emphasising the word. 'No guns, no screams, no feet running this way and that, no tanks rolling, no terrible explosions and fires. Not even someone tapping out Morse code. It's so . . . peaceful it hurts.'

Nancy wanted to touch him. Just to put her hand on his shoulder, perhaps, to let him know she understood what he meant, because she did and her eyes were suddenly stinging with tears. She stopped them in their tracks. The captain was highly sensitive to atmosphere, he mustn't see that she was upset.

His mood lightened suddenly. 'On,

the other hand,' he said, 'when I'm in my lonely room, especially at night, the silence drives me crazy. I can't read, no-one has thought to bring me a wireless.' Again came that wonderful smile. 'Perhaps they're afraid I might secretly tune in to Lord Haw Haw.'

Nancy laughed and the sad moment had passed.

'Would you like me to ask Matron about transferring you to a ward?' she asked. No matter what her own secret wish was, it was what was best for him that was important.

'Do you really think I'm ready for that?' he asked with a touch of his former sarcasm. 'I might throw a tantrum in the middle of the night, upset one of the night nurses perhaps. After all, there must have been a reason I was given the special privilege of a room to myself.'

'It's customary for every new patient,' Nancy informed him.

'But I've been here a few days now, and I'm bored. I long for human company, your visits are very welcome, Nurse Mellor, but I can't indulge in barrack room chat with you now, can I?'

Nancy laughed again. 'You're incorrigible,' she said. 'Right, I'm definitely asking Matron to move you. But if you can't sleep for the other men's snores, don't blame me.'

As she left him, she was hoping against hope that Aunt Helen would let him go into her ward. After all, there was that spare bed.

Now Nancy could really help to look after Captain James Wallace. He was in her mind when she awoke in the morning, and the last thing she thought of before she went to sleep at night. It was silly, she knew, he was engaged to be married to another woman. Because this woman hadn't yet had the decency to enquire after her fiancé's health, meant nothing.

As for the captain himself, despite Nancy's misgivings that he might have difficulty adjusting to the other men in the room, he fitted in perfectly. He became more mobile, anxious to help with the bedfast patients, indulging in ribaldry with the active ones, especially Angus, the young Scottish soldier. They spent some time in the dayroom playing cards and Nancy often heard their laughter.

They seemed to find no difficulty with the fact that Captain Wallace couldn't see the cards.

'I wouldn't cheat him,' Angus declared. 'You trust me, don't you, Jimmy?'

Nancy saw him wince at being called 'Jimmy', but he answered cheerfully enough, 'With my life, Angus, old boy.'

Then Angus was discharged and for a couple of days Captain Wallace seemed to mope about like a lost soul, but he soon picked up.

When Nancy went on a short spell of night duty, she found that Captain Wallace slept well and if one of the others awoke him, which sometimes happened; men had nightmares, who could blame them, he was sitting up awake, alert, asking, 'Can I do something, Nurse Mellor?'

One night, he was the one with insomnia and Nancy brought him some hot milk and sat by his bed, letting him talk quietly.

'When are they going to remove my bandages, Nurse?'

Nancy was sure the question was rhetorical and said nothing.

James Wallace went on, 'They come along, prodding and poking, peeking under the dressing, to see if they need changing presumably. I always squeeze my eyes tight shut. No sense in knowing any sooner than I have to if I'm never going to be able to see again.'

Nancy didn't know what to say. She did not know enough about the reason for the Captain's bandaged eyes and even if she had, she wouldn't have dreamed of offering him hope that might prove false.

He turned his head towards her, settling back comfortably on his pillows. 'I never felt it, you know. There was this almighty blast and then the lights went out. When I awoke in a field hospital my leg hurt like hell, excuse me, Nurse, and my eyes were under wraps. And here I am. I don't suppose there'll be any lasting damage to the leg, it's getting better every day, but the eyes ... Well, that's another matter entirely.'

The man in the next bed stirred restlessly. The captain dropped his voice to a low whisper.

'Thank you for the hot milk, Nurse Mellor. I think I'll be able to drop off now.'

Nancy stood up and picked up the empty glass from the bedside table. 'Are you sure you'll be all right, Captain?' she asked.

He nodded. 'Quite sure, thank you. By the way, my name is James, why don't you call me that? Anything is better than being addressed as Captain all the time.' He smiled in the darkness. 'So long as it's not Jimmy, of course.'

'I'd never call you Jimmy,' Nancy promised.

But she wouldn't be calling him James either. One had to remain formal, respectful. Aunt Helen, in her capacity as Matron did not encourage familiarity with the patients. Being friendly, helpful, a good listener, was one thing. But it wouldn't do to go around calling everybody by their first name. No way would Aunt Helen allow the soldiers to address the nurses by their christian names. Even cheerful Angus was always addressed as Sergeant Fraser.

But in her heart, Nancy knew she would always think of the Captain as James.

She felt as though she knew him so much more than she knew the other patients.

6

Nancy looked up from her position behind the nurses' station where she was finishing off some notes for Matron. Apart from the two bedfast patients who were snoozing off the effects of their lunch, the ward was empty at present and Nancy had taken the opportunity to catch up with some paperwork.

The sharp, staccato footsteps coming along the corridor towards the ward were not those of a nurse. No nurse would wear high heeled shoes. Whoever it was, she was walking with purpose and Nancy put down her pen and moved towards the door, just as a tall, slender woman wearing a dark fur coat came into view.

The fur coat was most appropriate to the weather as with the beginning of November it had turned cold and blustery with a strong northerly wind blowing off the lake, but the ward was very warm and as she saw Nancy, the woman started to unfasten the coat, pushing it back off her shoulders to reveal a floral patterned silky dress with a low plunging neckline.

She wore bright red lipstick and over wide set eyes of an almost violet shade, her eyebrows were plucked and arched. The drifting of some expensive and subtle perfume invaded Nancy's nostrils.

She had the air and beauty of a model and she gave Nancy a dazzling smile.

'Hello,' she greeted, 'I'm looking for Captain James Wallace.' She stared at the empty beds. 'Matron said I would find him here, so where is he?'

Her expression was pleasant but her voice slightly imperious to Nancy's ears. So this was the mysterious Nancy. Nancy tried to suppress the feeling of resentment that rose unbidden in her.

'Captain Wallace is taking a bath,

Miss . . . er . . . ?' she said.

'Miss Glenister. Nancy Glenister.' The eyebrows seemed to arch even further. 'Taking a bath? But I thought James was bedridden.'

Nancy smiled. 'No, no, not at all. He walks very well with the aid of a cane.'

'And his eyes? Surely his eyes . . . ?'

'Are still bandaged, Miss Glenister. An orderly has gone with him, of course.'

She remembered the fuss Captain Wallace had made about that and inwardly smiled.

'Even my nanny allowed me to take a bath alone,' he had protested.

'Oh, I see. Well I shall just have to wait, I suppose.' She looked around for somewhere to sit, but Nancy didn't want her disturbing the two sleeping men; she hadn't bothered to try to lower her voice.

'Would you come to the dayroom, Miss Glenister, and when Captain Wallace returns I'll bring him to you.'

'Very well.' She turned on her high

heels and stalked ahead of Nancy down the corridor, as though she knew where she was going.

Nancy couldn't resist asking as she caught the woman up, 'Are you a relative, Miss Glenister?'

She knew who the woman was, of course, but only because of her prior meeting with James Wallace on the train that day. Aunt Helen had only mentioned that he had a fiancée and he himself had never mentioned her name.

'James is my fiancé,' Miss Glenister announced.

Nancy dearly wanted to say, 'And why have you waited all this time to come and see him?' but that would have been disastrous and quite out of order.

They had reached the dayroom and Nancy stood to one side to allow the other woman to enter. Thankfully, there was no-one else in there.

As Miss Glenister took a seat in one of the comfortable chairs she pulled off her kid gloves and Nancy did not miss the huge solitaire engagement ring, or the scarlet painted nails.

'Would you like some tea, Miss Glenister?' she enquired politely.

'I would, thank you.' A brief smile flitted across the beautiful face. 'I've just returned from Scotland, only a couple of hours ago and the journey seemed endless. It was so cold in the Highlands, but I couldn't get out of it. Sir Archie Drummond was having one of his lavish shooting parties and you know how it is, one simply has to accept such an invitation however much one hates the idea.'

Does one? Nancy thought bitterly.

'My poor darling, James,' she cooed, 'I feel so bad about not being here when he needed me, but I honestly had no idea he would be arriving so soon, and by the time I got the word, I was in Scotland. Never mind, I've taken over a beautiful house, right on the lakeside so I'm hoping James will be able to join me there shortly, then I can help to nurse him back to health. I've engaged the services of an excellent local woman

81

to act as housekeeper.' Her smile was coy. 'All very proper, nurse.'

Then she suddenly seemed to realise that she was chattering away to a mere nurse and her expression froze.

'How about that tea, nurse?' she asked.

Nancy hurried away. She felt angry, unreasonably angry perhaps. She had almost felt like she should bob a curtsey to the woman. She was prejudiced, she knew.

As she approached the dayroom with the tea she heard voices coming through the partly open door.

'I don't know, Nancy! I don't know what condition my eyes will be in, how many times do I have to say it?'

James must have returned whilst she was making the tea and someone, Aunt Helen perhaps, had already told him his fiancée was here. Nancy hesitated, holding the tray out in front of her. She should make her presence known, but Miss Glenister was speaking now in a shrill, complaining voice and Nancy felt unable to move.

'But, James, this is merely a convalescent home. Surely patients here are well on the way to the recovery even before they arrive. Isn't that what convalescing means?'

'Who knows what anything means any more, Nancy.' James sounded tired, depressed.

At once Miss Glenister was all concern. 'Darling, don't be cross with me because I haven't been earlier. You know how concerned I am about you, but I simply couldn't get out of the trip to Scotland. When your bandages come off and you can see again you can come to the house I've rented. Oh, it's so beautiful, you'll love it, the garden leads right down to the lakeside. There's even a little boat, and Mrs Horsfall.'

James broke in sharply. 'I may never see again, Nancy. Hasn't that crossed your frivolous little mind?'

'You're so cruel, James.' There were tears in her voice now. 'I thought you'd be pleased about the house.'

'I am, darling, I am. Forgive me.'
Now the Captain was the one trying to give comfort. 'I'm so glad you're here, I've missed you so much.'

There was a long silence.

Nancy felt embarrassed, it was obvious they were kissing or at least holding one another.

She took a deep breath and marched as loudly as she could into the room. She saw them spring apart like children caught in an act of mischief.

'Why, Captain Wallace,' she cried, 'I've only brought one cup, do you want me to fetch another?'

'No thank you, Nurse Mellor. You've already met my fiancée, Miss Nancy Glenister, I presume.'

'Yes, I have.' Nancy put the tray on the small table.

'I don't really want the tea now, thank you nurse,' Miss Glenister told her in a cool voice. 'I'm going to take James for a stroll around the garden.' She turned to him. 'Where's your top coat, darling?'

'It's very cold,' Nancy told her, 'and if Captain Wallace has just come out of a hot bath . . . '

'Don't fuss, Nurse.' She turned her back on Nancy and she realised she had been effectively dismissed.

As she turned to the door James called out, 'Thank you, Nurse Mellor. Sorry about the tea.'

Nancy was trembling as she went back to the ward. She was beginning to feel an intense dislike for Miss Nancy Glenister.

But when she finally left and James Wallace came back on to the ward he was full of good spirits, his joy at meeting his fiancée again evident in every footfall, every word.

Later that night as the ward settled down and Nancy's shift came to an end, the Captain called her over to his bed.

'Would you do me a favour, Nurse?' he whispered.

'If I can,' Nancy said, wondering what she was going to be asked to do.

'Can you try and find out when the eye doctor is likely to put in an appearance? My patience is beginning to wear a little thin now and if he doesn't get a move on I shall tear the damned bandages off myself.'

'You mustn't think of doing something so rash, Captain Wallace,' she cried.

'No, well,' he turned his head away, 'maybe not but I need to know the truth. This suspense is killing me.'

He had never gone on like this before, not even in his worst moments. Nancy was in no doubt who had made him like that.

Even before the ophthalmic consultant came to Greystones, Captain James Wallace started to visit his fiancée's rented house.

'I felt I couldn't refuse permission,' Aunt Helen told Nancy when they were enjoying a cup of tea together in Aunt Helen's private sitting-room during a quiet moment. 'Miss Glenister is a very persuasive young lady. I cannot of course condone her absence for so long, but now that she's here, well she seems to be doing Captain Wallace a power of good. Don't you think so, Nancy?'

Aunt Helen had not heard the conversation in the dayroom and had obviously fallen under the woman's undoubted, though in Nancy's opinion, false charm.

'I'm sure he's very happy she's here, Aunt Helen,' was all she said.

'You don't look too happy yourself, Nancy. And, by the way, are you aware that Miss Glenister has the same Christian name as yourself?'

'Yes I am.' She didn't bother to let her aunt know that this was because of a chance meeting on a northbound train over two years ago.

Nancy did not mention either that James was concerned about and impatient for the eye doctor's visit. At the moment it seemed he was content to visit his fiancée's house as much as he could, but Nancy was secretly worried that he might be overdoing it.

It was a few days later, a cold wet day when there was a definite feel of winter in the air and even the odd flurry of snow, that Nancy was summoned to the telephone by one of the senior nurses, Staff Nurse Harper, a woman she liked and respected very much.

'There's a phone call for you, Nancy,' the staff nurse said, 'I think it's that young Captain. He sounded distressed.'

'James Wallace?' Nancy said sharply.

He had gone to his fiancée's house first thing that morning. She had arrived in a smart little sports car — it seemed she had at least two cars — and had promised to have James back by tea time. But it was now turned five and he was still out. Nancy felt uneasy because surely it wouldn't do him any good leaving a warm house and going out into the freezing night air.

She hurried to the phone and snatched up the receiver.

'Hello?' she said.

'Nurse Mellor, is that you?' his voice was hoarse.

'Yes, what is it, Captain?'

'Can you come and get me?'

'But . . . why, where's Miss Glenister?'

'I don't know. I've fallen and banged my face. I think I'm bleeding. Please come. I'm sitting on the floor, I knocked the telephone off the table when I fell. A good job I did, at least I was able to phone you.'

Nancy knew she shouldn't just dash off without telling anyone she was going and perhaps a male orderly might have come in useful, but she couldn't wait for that. James needed her. She had travelled up to the Lakes in her father's car, and though she used it frugally, she felt going to James's aid as quickly as she could was justified.

'I'm on my way, James,' she told him, thankful that she at least knew where the house was, as she had seen the address written in his records.

From that moment on, Nancy never called him, or thought of him as Captain Wallace again.

7

There was a faint light in one of the rooms, but the rest of the house seemed to be in complete darkness. There was no car parked outside, but that may only mean both Miss Glenister's cars were in the garage.

The snow was coming down quite heavily now. Nancy parked at the head of the drive and snatched up her medical bag, hoping against hope that the door would be unlocked. She knocked gently and turned the handle and the door opened at once.

'James?' she called out.

'I'm in here.' His voice came from a room on the right of the long, wide hall.

Where on earth was the housekeeper, Mrs Horsfall, Nancy wondered.

James was sitting with his back against the sofa, the phone at his side. Only the one lamp was lit and Nancy quickly switched on two more so she could see what state James was in. Immediately she noticed that the windows were uncurtained and the blackness of the night, the snowflakes settling on the window seemed to rush in at her.

She drew the curtains hurriedly, both the Black Out curtains and the chintzy floral drapes. Then she turned to James.

'Oh, James!' she cried when she saw the blood running down from a nasty gash on his right cheek, just below the cheekbone.

'How stupid of me,' he said, 'but I didn't know the layout of the furniture and nobody answered my calls. I have no idea where Nancy is or Mrs Horsfall either for that matter.'

Nancy got to work on the cut. Thankfully it didn't look as though it would need stitching.

'How long have you been on your own?' she asked.

'I didn't remember that either,' James said, wincing as the sting of the iodine hit him. 'I remember going for a nap earlier. I was shattered. I love Nancy dearly but she is such a chatterbox.'

He said these last words in an indulgent voice and Nancy could see, that even now, abandoned and bleeding and his fiancée goodness knows where, he could see no wrong in her actions. 'When I woke up the house was so quiet and I soon realised I was the only one home. Then when I came in here, after feeling my way downstairs, I tripped over a silly little table I think it was, or a pouffe or something, and banged my face on something else.'

Nancy saw it was indeed a table, lying now on its side, the green glass bowl that had been on it thankfully still intact.

'I hope you don't mind my calling you, Nurse Mellor,' James went on as she put sticking plaster over his cut. 'I asked the operator to put me through to the hospital and I thought, 'Better not ask for Matron; she might curtail my field trips. I knew you'd be discreet.'

'But I must report this, James,' she protested, helping him to his feet.

'But it's only a scratch. You said it didn't need stitching. I feel such a fool now. If I'd realised I wasn't bleeding to death I wouldn't have phoned at all, but I didn't know how badly hurt I was. I could feel the blood running down my face and I suppose I panicked.'

Was it any wonder, Nancy thought. She closed her bag with a sharp click.

'It's probably reached Matron's ears by now anyway,' she told him.

He groaned. 'So I'll be sent to bed without any supper, I suppose.'

Nancy laughed. She was beginning to feel relieved. It had been such a shock, she had had no idea in what condition she would find him.

'I think it's more than likely Miss Glenister will be the one in for a scolding,' she said.

She didn't miss the tightening of James' lips and wished she hadn't said that.

'She knew I was asleep. Perhaps she

just popped out for a minute. What time is it, nurse?'

Nancy looked at her watch. 'Twenty to six,' she said.

'My goodness, it was only just after lunch when I went upstairs, so where is she? Do you think there's been an accident?'

'No, I'm quite sure there hasn't.' She was trying to reassure him but if Miss Glenister had gone out in her car and bearing in mind that the snow had started to come down much earlier in the day, anything was possible, she supposed.

It was then that she noticed the white envelope propped up on the mantelpiece, above the dying log fire that somebody had obviously lit earlier. With annoyance she also noticed there was no guard at the fire. The word *James* was scrawled across the front of the envelope in a childish, feminine hand.

'I think Miss Glenister has left you a note,' Nancy said.

'A note?' James repeated. 'Then read it to me, Nurse. Please,' he added belatedly.

Nancy felt uncomfortable opening the envelope and unfolding the sheet of faintly scented writing paper. This would be the second time she had read something that was not intended for her eyes.

'*Darling*,' she read, '*you are sleeping so soundly and look so warm and safe I haven't the heart to disturb you. I've gone to Ambleside with David Rattigan. You remember David, don't you, James? I told him I'd taken this house and he's wasted no time in dashing up here to see me. Well, to see us both really. We won't be long. Lots of kisses, Nancy.*'

Once more Nancy spoke without thinking. 'And just how did your fiancée think you were going to be able to read the note?'

'She must have asked Mrs Horsfall to read it to me,' James replied shortly. 'And where is she?'

His explanation didn't convince Nancy. It must have been obvious that James would not only be unable to find the note but to read it, so why bother writing it in the first place?

She could just have told her housekeeper where she was going.

Nancy thought a more likely explanation was that the ever-ebullient Miss Glenister had simply rattled off the note and never given a thought to James being unable to find it.

Which seemed to suggest to her probably suspicious mind, no doubt, that Mrs Horsfall had not been at the house when this David Rattigan arrived.

Only a few minutes later, the housekeeper confirmed this. She arrived with a shivery bustle as Nancy was pouring out some tea she had made for them both. She stared in surprise when she saw Nancy, melting snowflakes dripping off her sensible blue hat.

'Oh, good afternoon . . . Nurse,' she said, taking in Nancy's uniform.

Before Nancy could speak James

broke in sharply, 'Mrs Horsfall? Where have you been, woman? It wasn't a very wise move leaving me alone in a house I scarcely know, was it?'

Mrs Horsfall looked from one to the other of them in amazement. 'But, Captain Wallace, it was my half-day off today. I've been at my sister's, only a short walk away. Miss Glenister knew where I'd gone.' She looked around her. 'Where is she?'

Nancy spoke before James could. 'She's gone to Ambleside . . . With a friend.'

'Well, I never,' Mrs Horsfall tutted, removing her hat pin and shaking off the remaining snow from her hat. 'She shouldn't have done that. Leaving poor Captain Wallace alone.'

Nancy could see that she was deeply offended. 'No-one's blaming you, Mrs Horsfall,' Nancy said.

James had turned towards her and even without seeing his eyes, she could tell he wasn't pleased she seemed to be taking over.

'Take me back to the hospital, Nurse,' he said. 'I'll speak to Nancy later. Be so good, Mrs Horsfall, as to inform my fiancée when she finally shows up that I have left.'

'Of course, Captain, of course,' Mrs Horsfall gushed looking bewildered, as well she might.

It was then she seemed to notice the plaster on James' face for the first time.

'Good gracious me, you've hurt yourself!' she cried.

'It's nothing. Come on, Nurse Mellor, let's go. My coat's in the hall.'

The ground was slippery and James' steps were uncertain. He had stopped using his stick days ago and leaned heavily on her, but Nancy didn't mind.

Nancy Glenister came to Greystones early the next afternoon. Nancy was helping a couple of the men choose books in the small but well-stocked library and saw her parking her car outside. The large dark car this time, she noticed. The snow had stopped falling almost as soon as it had started, and there was only a thin covering, but it was bitterly cold.

She saw Nancy looking out of the window and came straight into the library. The men turned to stare at her admiringly, eyeing her up and down.

'I'm so glad I've seen you, Nurse. I understand James has had a slight accident,' she began, 'Do you know anything about it? Mrs Horsfall was in quite a state.'

'I went to your house,' Nancy told her, 'after receiving a telephone call from Ja, er, Captain Wallace. He had fallen and cut his face. Not badly, as it happened, but I'm sure your house-keeper gave you all the details.'

'Yes, she did.' Miss Glenister shrugged her elegant shoulders. 'I didn't know you were the nurse present, of course, and I suppose I should thank you. My absence was unavoidable, I'm afraid. The snow was frightening and David, Major Rattigan, tried two or three telephone kiosks but none of them worked, so I couldn't get a message to James.

'I fully expected Mrs Horsfall to have returned to the house before James awoke anyway, but, there you are.' She gave Nancy a bright smile. 'No harm done!' She tugged off her gloves. 'Is James up and about?'

'He's with the doctor at the moment,' Nancy said.

'Is he really? Does that mean what I think it means?'

'I doubt it. It isn't the ophthalmic specialist he's seeing.'

Miss Glenister heaved a long sigh. 'Oh, well, surely that happy day must come before long. When it does, Nurse Mellor, I want to be informed immediately. I will need to see James. Ideally I would like to be with him when the bandages are removed. Do you think that would be possible?'

'I have no idea, Miss Glenister. That is surely up to Captain Wallace and his doctor.'

'I suppose so.' Without another word, she turned and walked out of the library.

Each time she met Miss Glenister, Nancy was left quivering with anger. There was something about her that was positively loathsome and quite honestly she could not see what James saw in her. Was it a family thing perhaps? Wealthy parents who had desired a union between the two families. Whatever it was, James was obviously besotted by his fiancée and it frightened Nancy.

Especially as she was quickly coming to realise that she, too, had feelings for him.

This was the first time she had admitted that fact to herself and she pulled herself together.

James returned from his visit to the doctor with a broad smile on his face.

'Good news?' Nancy asked him, her heart skipping a beat.

'Very good news. My bandages come off tomorrow.' Then his mouth seemed to tremble. 'But is it good news, Nurse Mellor, or will it turn out to be the worst possible news?'

'You must have faith, Captain,' Nancy told him brightly.

He nodded. 'Yes, I must.'

'Did you see Miss Glenister?'

'I did.' Once more the smile returned. 'She was just in time to hear the news. The doctor allowed her to come into the consulting room. I hadn't the heart to be cross with her for leaving me yesterday, she was so sorry about it.'

Nancy said nothing but continued to fold the pile of clean pillow cases that someone had dumped on the nurses' station.

'She's coming again tomorrow. She wants to be with me when the bandages come off.'

'Yes, she told me,' Nancy said.

'She did?' he sounded surprised that this had been discussed. 'Of course Dr Fisher said it wasn't really up to him, but Nancy was adamant she would be here. By nine o'clock she said. The unveiling is at ten. Just think, nurse, I could be leaving here soon. My leg's improved tremendously and there'll be nothing to keep me here, will there? Nancy and I will probably stay at the lakeside house for a while till I find my feet again, so to speak, and then, hopefully I'll be shipped back to Europe.'

Hopefully? Nancy couldn't bear the thought of James returning to the Front, possibly to be hurt again and next time he might not be so lucky. But she could tell by the tone of his voice that the thought of being hurt a second time simply had not entered his head. He wanted to go back. Well, she didn't want him to and she was quite sure his fiancée didn't.

'You've been wonderful, Nurse,' James said suddenly and then moved closer to her, catching hold of her shoulders and pulling her into his arms then kissing her cheek.

The remaining bedfast patient in the otherwise deserted ward sent up a loud cheer and James turned his head in that direction.

'Sorry, old boy, I thought we were alone,' he said.

He turned back to Nancy. 'Perhaps I shouldn't have done that.'

'That's all right.'

It wasn't the first time a grateful patient had kissed her. But now it was different. Nancy had felt James' warm lips on her cheek; felt his arms holding her and she was overcome by a rush of emotion because it was all so hopeless.

He would be all right, of course, she truly believed that, but once he was able to see he would be leaving Greystones, there would not be anything to keep him there, and she would probably never see him again.

He and Nancy Glenister would be married one day — would they wait till the end of the war she wondered? — she had a feeling Miss Glenister would not want a hurried war time wedding, but a lavish glittery affair when peace finally came, but she could be wrong about that.

8

Nancy slept badly that night. She was imagining James, too, tossing and turning in his bed. His whole future depended on what happened when his bandages came off.

And how would Miss Glenister be faring? Would she too be unable to sleep, thinking about tomorrow, praying for James? Or would she be with her friend, Major Rattigan, dancing the night away.

The thought was unworthy of her, Nancy realised. Of course James' fiancée would be worried. She wouldn't be human if she weren't.

The next morning dawned cold and clear. From her bedroom window Nancy could see the hills covered in their coating of icing sugar. The snow would be one of the first things that James would see perhaps. Oh, how she wished she could be there when it happened. Instead, it would be the other Nancy, who took his arm, who walked with him to the window and rejoiced at his childish delight.

She performed her early morning duties mechanically, unable to give them her full concentration, continually looking at her watch. James had been up even earlier than she was, his bed was empty and a passing orderly told her he had been taken to the library.

'The Captain didn't want any breakfast,' the orderly told her. 'He only wants to be notified as soon as Miss Glenister arrives.'

It was whilst she was helping another nurse to change the beds that Matron came into the ward. Her face was solemn. Once again Nancy glanced sharply at her fob watch. It was only half-past nine, so there couldn't be bad news about James.

'Nurse Mellor,' Matron said, 'could I possibly have a word with you? She smiled at the other nurse.' Ask Nurse

Phillips to give you a hand would you, Nurse Rhodes?'

Nancy followed Matron out of the ward. Neither of them spoke as they walked along the corridors to Matron's office. Nancy dare not speak, she didn't want to know what was wrong, because it was obvious that something was.

As soon as they had both sat down, Matron, now Aunt Helen in Nancy's mind, steeped her fingers and regarded Nancy with solemn eyes.

'I am rather concerned about a letter I have received this morning. Nancy,' she began, 'it was apparently delivered by hand even before it was light, but only came into my hands about fifteen minutes ago. You know the incoming post is sometimes delayed on its journey to me, which, of course, I don't condemn.' She paused and Nancy wanted to urge her on but simply sat, listening to the thumping of her heart, but she was certain whoever that letter was from it had something to do with James.

Matron opened the top drawer of her desk and took out a slim envelope. Nancy's heart gave a leap as she recognised the same writing paper she had seen in Miss Glenister's house and breathed in the same faint scent of roses. The envelope had a slightly bulky look as though it contained some object.

Matron pushed it towards Nancy. It was clearly addressed to Matron, Greystones Convalescent Home with the words Private and Confidential scrawled in the top left hand corner. Nancy Glenister's childish handwriting, there was no doubt of that.

'But why is Miss Glenister writing to you, Aunt Helen?' she asked, alarm bells starting to ring.

'Of course, you know her writing from the other day,' Aunt Helen said.

Nancy felt herself blushing, remembering her aunt's displeasure when she had been told of Nancy's unauthorised visit to the house, though she had eventually accepted her explanation for that.

'Yes,' Nancy mumbled, 'it's the same paper Miss Glenister used to write her note to Captain Wallace.'

'I'm sure you're right, because the letter inside this envelope addressed to myself is also from Miss Glenister, but the other letter, the one I haven't opened is addressed to Captain Wallace.'

Nancy waited for her aunt to explain; by now her hands were clenched together in her lap because she had a terrible sinking feeling that she knew what was coming next.

'I will read my letter, Nancy.' She unfolded the sheet of paper, and reached for her reading glasses.

'*Dear Matron, I am writing to you because I do not know how else to handle this dreadful dilemma in which I find myself. It is with sadness that I must tell you I cannot consider myself to be engaged to Captain James Wallace any longer. This has not been an easy decision to make, I have struggled with my conscience long and* hard, but I have completely made up my mind.

'You may think me a coward, perhaps I am, but I cannot wait to find out if James' eyes will be all right, and I cannot tell him of my decision in person. I am enclosing a letter for James, together with my engagement ring. I leave it entirely up to you, Matron, as to whether you open and read the other letter before you speak to James. I pray that once his bandages are removed, he will be able to read the letter for himself. I have given him my reasons for breaking off our engagement in full, and asked him not to try to contact me. In any case, I shall be sailing for America in a day's time.

'I will say no more to you, Matron. Perhaps you will wonder why I did not at least wait to see if James' sight was undamaged, but I thought it better to make a clean break before I am faced with another worse decision to make, that of deserting James knowing he will never see again.

'*Please accept my apologies. I pray that both James, and yourself, will be able to forgive me one day.*

Yours sincerely, Nancy Glenister.'

Aunt Helen put the letter down and removed her glasses. 'So, Nancy, what do we do?' She asked sadly.

Nancy's eyes were blinded with tears. She tried to fight them back, but the sobs broke from her, she could not stop herself. At once, Aunt Helen was out of her chair, coming round to Nancy to put an arm around her shaking shoulders.

'My dear child!' was all she said.

Nancy sniffed and found a handkerchief in her skirt pocket, dabbing at her eyes, trying to bring herself under control.

'I'm sorry, Aunt Helen,' she said.

'No need for apologies, I know how fond you have grown of Captain Wallace. We all have. He is a very brave man.'

'But this will destroy him, he loves her so much.'

111

'He had talked to you about his feelings for Miss Glenister?' Aunt Helen's voice was very quiet.

Nancy looked up at her. There was a slightly disturbed expression on her aunt's face.

'Sometimes, yes, he has,' she admitted.

'Nancy, you know you cannot get involved with any patient.'

'I am aware of that, Matron,' Nancy said formally, 'but we are only human, aren't we?'

Aunt Helen smiled. 'Of course, but now I need your advice, Nancy, because I must confess I don't know what to do.'

In the end they decided to leave things until they knew the outcome of James' visit to the specialist. Nancy went back to her duties. She felt she had given herself away to her aunt. She was devastated about Nancy Glenister's betrayal, but in her heart she was not really surprised and felt that in the long run, James would be better off without her. Of course, he would not see it that way. He would be heartbroken, even if he discovered he still had perfect vision, the blow would be vicious.

Ten o'clock came and went and Nancy's thoughts were constantly with James. He would be sitting there as the bandages were unwrapped, waiting, waiting for that moment when there was no longer any restrictions between his eyes and the truth that must be faced, no matter what it was. And after that, well then there was also the truth about his fiancée to face.

Nancy knew that Aunt Helen would be there with James, but when she had asked if she could be present she had been told most definitely, 'That would not be appropriate, Nancy, Mr Slater, the ophthalmic consultant will have his own nurse in attendance. As soon as I know anything, one way or the other, you will be the first to hear it.'

Nancy had to be content with that. But when she eventually saw Matron, much later in the morning, her nerves were at screaming point. She heard the familiar footsteps echoing along the corridor. Only Matron had that particular tread. Nancy dashed out of the door of the ward. One look at Matron's face told her all she needed to know.

'He's all right!' she cried; it wasn't a question.

Aunt Helen nodded. 'Yes, Nurse Mellor, he's all right. A little disorientated at present, but that will pass. Mr Slater doesn't think Captain Wallace will ever have the keen vision he had before and will probably have to wear spectacles, but he can see.'

Relief flooded over Nancy.

'Oh, thank goodness. But does he know, about Miss Glenister I mean?'

Matron nodded. 'He does. I took him into my study and showed him the letters, mine and his. He opened his whilst I was there, but naturally I didn't probe him as to its contents.'

'And?'

'He asked to be taken immediately to Miss Glenister's rented house. It wasn't

114

something I would have recommended, but I didn't see how I could stop him. He will be free to leave the Home in a few days time. An orderly drove him down there but he wanted to be alone. Who came blame him?'

Aunt Helen's words were buzzing around Nancy's head. If James was discharged she would never see him again. Perhaps he wouldn't be allowed back to the Front, but at the very least he would be rejoining his regiment. It was more than she could bear.

She turned and walked, not back into the ward but along the corridor and on to the staffs' private quarters, disregarding her aunt's cry of, 'Nancy, come back!' She reached her own room and shut the door behind her, going to stand by the window, seeing the same view that James would see, but what would it mean to him now that he had lost his Nancy?

A sharp rap on the door was followed by her aunt's entrance. 'Nancy, it is highly irregular of you to leave your duties in that fashion.'

Nancy turned. Her aunt's expression was a mixture of concern and annoyance.

'Yes, I'm sorry, Aunt Helen,' Nancy apologised.

'Your anxiety over Captain Wallace does you credit, but I can't help thinking that you are going a little too far. He will have to come to terms with what his fiancée has done, but at least the terrible affliction of blindness has been taken from him and that surely must count for something.'

Nancy wanted to believe those words, but she knew James, she knew how hard he would be taking Miss Glenister's rejection, so hard that probably the restoration of his sight, would be of secondary importance to him.

'I want to go to him, Aunt Helen,' she said. 'Oh, not now, when I come off duty I mean.'

'What you do in your spare time is your own affair, Nancy,' Aunt Helen said quietly, 'but I would strongly advise against any such move. He needs time to himself. He has a great deal of adjusting to do.'

'But I presume he will be coming back here before he is actually discharged. I need to see him before that. You see, it's quite possible that when he sees me for the first time he will remember that we have met before.'

Aunt Helen looked surprised. 'And when was this? You never said . . . '

'It was before the war. We met on a train. I was coming home for Dad's funeral and James was going to join his regiment in Catterick.'

'So Captain Wallace is 'James' to you, is he, Nancy?'

'I never address him by his christian name,' Nancy said quickly, knowing that she had, that night at the house.

She said no more, there didn't seem to be much else she could say.

Aunt Helen came further into the room, speaking now in a kindly voice. 'My advise to any nurse who had feelings for a patient, would always be 'tread softly', but I can see what Captain Wallace means to you. Can you be discreet, can you tell yourself first and foremost that he is a man who was engaged to be married, who has been dealt a dreadful blow?'

Nancy nodded her head.

'Then go and see him. He may, after all, welcome you.' She turned and walked out of the room.

Nancy sank down on to the edge of the bed, feeling a sense of great relief. She looked at her watch. Only one hour to go. Could James wait that long?

This time, the door to the lakeside house was locked and Nancy rang the bell, expecting Mrs Horsfall to come and answer it. She had changed out of her uniform and now wore her red winter coat with a matching tam o'shanter pulled on to her head, warm woollen mittens on her hands.

When the door opened and James stood there she was taken aback.

'Hello,' she said.

James frowned, momentarily thrown by the change of outfit. He appeared dishevelled, wearing no tie, his hair looking as though he had run his fingers through it several times. Seeing those warm brown eyes again brought Nancy's feelings for this man to the fore. She wanted to put her arms around him and hold him close; he looked so sad and . . . lost.

'It's me,' she said, 'Nurse Mellor.'

'Oh? Come in.' James turned away from the door, proceeding Nancy down the hall and into the room she had been in on her last visit.

Now it was daylight outside, with a pale, wintry sun filtering into the room. The fire was almost out and the room felt cold.

'Why have you come, Nurse Mellor?' James spoke with his back to her, standing in front of the window, staring blankly at the chilly garden. 'Have you heard the news, is that it? And I don't mean about my eyes. I mean about Nancy. Does news, good and bad, travel as fast in a hospital as it does anywhere else?'

'Yes, Aunt Helen told me.'

'Aunt Helen?' Still he didn't turn and look at her.

'Matron is my aunt.'

He did turn then, screwing up his eyes as though the light through the windows had hurt them, which was possible considering he hadn't been able to see anything for quite sometime.

'Really?' A cold smile touched his mouth.

This was the same James who had first arrived at Greystones. Depressed, frightened, unsure of what the future might hold for him.

'Do . . . do you need anything?' she asked him.

What a stupid question she immediately thought.

James must think so too because he laughed harshly. 'There is a great deal I need, Nurse Mellor, but a good bedside manner and a soothing hand upon my brow isn't going to provide it.'

He moved away from the window, coming towards her, looking at her intently. Then without warning he reached up and snatched off the tam o'shanter, so that Nancy's dark hair came tumbling over her shoulders. Recognition dawned at last.

'Nancy,' he said.

9

Nancy built up the fire, using the logs in the wicker basket on the hearth. James made coffee.

She had asked him, 'Where's Mrs Horsfall?'

'I sent her home until tomorrow morning. Don't worry, I was very polite and I think she rather liked the idea of a few hours extra off. My . . . ex fiancée can be a tartar as far as domestic staff are concerned.'

Nancy didn't doubt it. They hadn't said much yet. James had quickly disappeared into the kitchen, calling to Nancy to see if she could breathe some life into the dying logs, which she was pleased to find she could. When he returned with a tray, bearing two ill-matching mugs and a sugar bowl from which grains of sugar had spilled over the side, Nancy went and took it from him.

He sat down staring at her. 'Did you know all along it was me?' he asked.

She sat opposite, warming her fingers around the mug. 'Not at first. When Matron mentioned your name I only thought it sounded familiar, but as soon as I saw you, spoke to you, I knew.'

'Yet, you said nothing. You must have known I was at a disadvantage, but I'm sure if you'd jogged my memory I would have been able to remember you. After all, we talked at some length on that northbound train.'

So they had; it seemed a long time ago but clear in her memory as though it were only yesterday . . .

'You were going home for your father's funeral as I recall?' His voice was very formal, cold even. When he had spoken her name earlier, it had been with softness, gentleness but all that was gone now.

'Yes.'

'I don't remember your telling me you were a nurse. Perhaps if I had I would have known who you were much earlier. Even before I could see you.'

'No, what I did for a living was never mentioned,' Nancy agreed, sipping her drink.

He had left his untouched.

'But you weren't a nurse here at Greystones, before the war, were you? From what I've gleaned, this place used to be a private house.'

Nancy nodded. 'My Aunt Helen's house, yes. She had it converted to a convalescent home just before the war started. I was a nurse in London when I first met you, then I did further training at the Leeds General Infirmary after my father died. I came here in October.'

James's eyebrows rose. 'As recently as that? Then, we mightn't have met at all.'

That was true. Would it perhaps have been better if they hadn't? No, she wouldn't believe that; she couldn't.

'Quite a coincidence, you might say, that we should meet up again.' He picked up his mug then and drank some of the coffee, putting it down almost immediately and pulling a face. 'I never could make a decent mug of coffee,' he remarked.

'Perhaps it's not very good coffee in the first place, there is a war on you know.' She smiled at him.

He didn't return her smile. 'You can rest assured, Nurse Mellor that my ex fiancée would only purchase the good stuff.'

There was an awkward silence.

Nancy spoke impulsively, 'I'm so sorry, James.'

She saw his hands bunch into tight fists.

'She's done it before,' he said. 'Well, perhaps not gone quite so far as she has this time, crossing the ocean to get away from me, but ours has been a stormy relationship from the beginning.'

Her voice was quiet, 'Please, won't you call me Nancy?' she pleaded.

She wasn't prepared for his rush of anger. 'How can I do that? How can I mention her name? . . . Can't you see what she's done to me?'

He bent his head forward and covered his eyes with his hand.

Nancy jumped up, crying out, 'Don't say that, don't ever say that! You're not the first person to lose a loved one during this awful war and you won't be the last. You should be thanking God for your sight, not feeling sorry for yourself.'

He looked at her then and slowly he smiled, a faint smile, but nevertheless it brought light to his eyes. Nancy sat down again abruptly.

'You're so right, Nurse ... sorry, Nancy. I have a great deal to be thankful for. They won't let me go back to Europe, you know. They expect me to take on a desk job, London probably and I shall need glasses with lenses like sweet jar bottoms, if I am to be able to cross a road without being knocked down by a bus, but at least I can see.'

He paused, looking thoughtful, remembering something.

'About that letter I was writing on

the train that day. That was to her. We'd been at a party and David Rattigan was there. She flirted with him outrageously. He's a major now, due for even higher promotion, that's why he's gone to Washington. Anyway, Nancy and I parted under a cloud. Hence the attempt to write that letter.'

'Did you ever finish it?' she asked.

'No, she wrote to me first, throwing herself on my mercy, telling me how much she loved me and asking me to forgive her. I wrote to her later and asked her to marry me. And the rest of this sorry tale you know.'

But James didn't know she still had the unfinished letter. She decided to tell him the truth. She didn't know what his reaction would be but did not expect the genuine laughter that burst out of him.

'You sentimental old thing!' he cried. Then, after a moment of silence whilst they both watched the flames of the now blazing fire, and the sky started to darken outside, Nancy said she should be making her way back to Greystones.

James said, 'I'm glad you came, Nancy, and I'm sorry my reception was less than welcoming.' He stood up and so did she. James looked out of the window, 'We'd better either be leaving or pulling on the black outs,' he said. 'Is that your car, by the way?'

She nodded.

'Then may I beg a lift from you? I intend to move in here later, at least until they ship me out, so to speak, but I feel I should have a word with Matron, with your Aunt Helen, before I do so. The rent is apparently paid on this place till the end of December and I can always pay more, if necessary.' He smiled, a slow, lazy smile that made Nancy's heart ache. 'Christmas in the Lakes, perhaps?'

★ ★ ★

On the 7th December the Japanese attacked Pearl Harbour and the United

States of America entered the war. It was a great talking point at the Home, but James did not join in these discussions. Or at least, Nancy never heard him do so on the days he visited. It was as though he had effectively cut himself off from the war.

Nor did he talk about Nancy Glenister. Unfortunately the news of his fiancée's betrayal, as James had predicted, spread like wildfire and the other men who had got to know James since his arrival at Greystones, and who liked him very much, were naturally sympathetic towards him.

He moved into the lakeside house soon after he was issued with his new spectacles. Nancy first saw him when she was pushing a patient back from the library. James suddenly appeared in the doorway of ward 7, where the soldiers he knew best were situated.

'Well, how do I look?' he asked cheerfully.

The man in the wheelchair sat back and studied him. 'Like a ruddy film star, mate,' he said in his strong London accent.

James laughed and looked tentatively at Nancy.

'Who do you think I look like, Nurse?' he asked.

He looked like James. A different James, an older James perhaps, and the tortoiseshell frames did tend to give him a distinguished look, but to her he looked wonderful.

'They suit you,' she told him and continued to push the chair along the corridor, afraid that if she stood there any longer she would give her feelings away, and she couldn't do that.

What James did when he was in the house she did not know but he slept there every night and spent a great deal of his time there. He grumbled affectionately about Mrs Horsfall who seemed to have taken him under her wing.

'She's like my mother,' James told Nancy, 'and her opinion of my ex-fiancée is not something a good lady like Mrs Horsfall should ever utter, but she cooks like an angel, even amidst rationing. I'm thinking of enlisting her,' he grinned, 'maybe 'press ganging' her would be a better way to describe it, and taking her down south with me when I leave.'

Nancy's heart missed a beat. 'Do you know when that will be?' she asked him.

'I've no idea, the army is being its usual cagey self, but I shall go when I'm told to and go where I'm told to, I suppose.'

He did not sound too happy at the prospect.

The days of December seemed to fly by. They had some more snow and bets were being taken on the possibility of a White Christmas.

On the 21st December they held a candlelight carol service. Nancy's eyes filled with tears as she heard the predominately male voices singing *Silent Night, Holy Night*.

On that day, too, a parcel arrived for her and when she opened it, she found a gaily wrapped package, soft and mysterious with a card attached.

To Nancy, with all my love, Alec. Hope you are well. I miss you.

She tried to be pleased with Alec's thoughtfulness, but it seemed that he was still trying to win her.

And now there was James, who occupied her mind and her heart.

She put the gift in her top drawer, and threw the outer brown paper wrapper away, telling herself she wouldn't open it till Christmas morning, but somehow she doubted that she would ever open it.

To everybody's delight, snow began falling on Christmas Eve, as though on cue, soft white flakes that fluttered from the still sky. People stood at the windows watching it fall and groans went up when Black Out time came round.

Nancy was helping to serve afternoon tea, wartime scones prepared lovingly in the kitchen, and the ever present jellies, when Matron called her to her study.

Nancy was feeling a bit low, here it was, Christmas Eve at last, and James had not bothered to show up.

She worried that he might be feeling lonely and depressed; all the men felt the absence of their loved ones, and their wartime comrades who had fallen in battle, more acutely at this time.

Aunt Helen was smiling. 'You're to go to Captain Wallace's house,' she declared. 'He's just telephoned. His good housekeeper has apparently prepared a Christmas feast for him, far too much for one man, Captain Wallace told me, and he's asked permission for you to join him. Would you like to?'

Would she? Of course she would but she felt she had to say, 'Wouldn't Captain Wallace prefer to join us here, Aunt Helen? And why is he having his Christmas dinner tonight?'

'I don't suppose he wishes to incur the displeasure of the redoubtable Mrs Horsfall. It would be a brave man who would do that, Nancy. And to answer your other question, I suspect the

Captain intends having two Christmas dinners this year.'

So did that mean James would be at Greystones tomorrow? And was he asking her to join him tonight merely to help him consume the Christmas dinner, Nancy thought ruefully? Whatever, she wasn't going to miss this opportunity to be alone with him.

Because of the falling snow, Nancy decided to walk to the lakeside house; it wasn't so far and she knew the route well by now. She was muffled up in her cheerful red coat with the collar turned up. She hadn't left Greystones for a couple of days and she was surprised how deeply biting the cold was. When she arrived, she was shivering, and wet with melting snow.

James let her in, throwing the door open wide. 'Nancy, oh, you poor girl,' he cried, 'let's get you out of that wet coat.'

'Merry Christmas, James,' Nancy greeted him, looking round for Mrs Horsfall who, if she was home, usually appeared as soon as the door was opened.

'Are we alone?' she asked as James helped her off with her coat.

He looked at her solemnly. 'Does that bother you, Nancy?'

A hot flush stained her cold cheeks. 'No, of course not.'

'Mrs Horsfall has gone home to her family. She has apparently a brood of children and grandchildren, all requiring her presence more than we do, at this season of the year.'

He led her into the sitting room. 'I thought we'd eat in here,' he said, 'so much more cosy than the formal dining room.' He waved his hand with a flourish, and Nancy saw the small table in front of the cheery log fire, the crisp white tablecloth, the candles, the gleaming cutlery and glassware. Even a bottle of wine.

'Home-made parsnip wine, so heaven alone knows what it will taste like,' James told her. 'Our meal is keeping warm in the oven. A roast chicken from

Mrs Horsfall's farmer neighbour or should I say part of one, roast potatoes, mashed swede, onion gravy and, the pièce de résistance . . . portions of Mrs Horsfall's precious Christmas pudding.'

It sounded wonderful. A veritable feast!

'But first,' James went on, 'a little music.'

He went to a gramophone in the corner of the room and set up a record, a hissing record admittedly of a deep tenor voice singing *Danny Boy*.

The scene was set and suddenly Nancy felt nervous. To relieve her tension she produced James' Christmas present from her handbag.

He looked surprised. 'For me?' he asked.

Nancy nodded shyly. 'Nothing very much,' she said.

It was only a box of linen handkerchiefs that she had purchased in Windermere. Boring, she knew . . .

'I shall open it after we've eaten, Nancy,' he told her, walking to a bureau and picking up a small parcel wrapped in holly sprigged paper.

'Not to be outdone, here is your gift,' he said.

She was touched. 'Thank you,' she said.

He was a wonderful host, attentive, amusing, waiting on her. Had he been like this with the other Nancy, she wondered? She couldn't really imagine Miss Glenister eating at a small card table, drinking totally bland homemade parsnip wine, but to her, the meal was a banquet and she wouldn't have changed it for the most expensive meal in a plush West End restaurant.

After they had eaten, Nancy started to collect the dirty dishes.

'What are you doing, Nancy?' James asked.

'I'm going to wash up,' she said.

'Over my dead body.' James rose immediately. 'You are a guest tonight. You've tended me over these past weeks with loving care, now it's my turn to lavish some attention on you.' He grinned. 'Anyway, all I'm going to do is pile the dirty crocks in the sink.' He raised his hand for silence as Nancy started to protest. 'I have had strict instructions from Mrs Horsfall that not a pot must be washed. She will do it all in the morning, Christmas Day or no Christmas Day . . . I wasn't going to argue with her.'

Nancy didn't really feel comfortable with that but decided to let it go. At least for the time being!

When every last dish was cleared away, James joined Nancy in the sitting-room. She saw that he was not wearing his glasses.

'You've taken your glasses off,' she said.

'I don't really need them indoors,' he told her. He joined her on the settee. 'I can see you very clearly, Nancy and you look very lovely.'

'Thank you,' she murmured.

Then he turned her head towards him and kissed her softly on the mouth.

'A very Merry Christmas.'

'I think we've already said that.'

He was very close; Nancy could feel the heat from the fire and the parsnip wine, bland or not, was having a strange affect on her.

'I should be thanking you, Nancy,' James said softly. 'You've helped me so much since . . . well . . . since my world fell apart, I suppose. You above everyone else has made me see I still have so much to live for. You've scolded me when I wanted to feel sorry for myself, you've listened to my moans. It means so much to me, Nancy.'

She wanted to tell him it was because she loved him, but knew she couldn't. She knew that he was still in love with the other Nancy. She would be there for James and she was glad he felt he could trust and rely on her. She would not ask for more.

It was very late when she finally realised it was time to drag herself away. They had played more gramophone records, James insisting on dancing with her and turning out to be an excellent dancer. He held her close, his hand warm upon her back. They laughed a lot and at times simply sat staring into the fire, listening to the crackling of the logs, content just to enjoy the peace and quiet.

Then they opened their gifts. James was delighted with his handkerchieves.

'Just what I wanted,' he assured her.

He had bought Nancy a small pewter brooch in the shape of a wren. It was beautiful. James pinned it to the collar of her blouse.

'I saw it in a little shop,' he said, 'and I thought 'That's perfect for Nancy'.'

She knew, whatever other presents she may receive, nothing would mean the same as that brooch.

Then Nancy remembered. 'There's a midnight service at the local church,' she announced.

'Then we will go.' James jumped to his feet. 'And afterwards I'll walk you back to the Home.'

'You don't have to do that,' Nancy said.

'But, I do, the streets are pitch black you know.'

As it turned out, the sky was clear with a bright moon and lots of stars. Other people were heading for the church, including some from Grey- stones with nurses pushing wheelchairs through the snow. The church was lit by candles and decorated with holly and white lilies. As they took their seats, Nancy saw Aunt Helen further down the church. She was turning in her seat looking in their direction.

Nancy gave a little wave and Aunt Helen smiled and inclined her head. The service began with the singing of *O' Little Town of Bethlehem*. Those that were able rose to their feet. Nancy saw that James, who was now wearing his glasses again, was peering closely at his hymn sheet, but his voice was clear and pleasant. As the carol ended, the congregation sat down again.

'Let us pray,' the vicar said.

The congregation bowed their heads, and the vicar began to speak. James reached for Nancy's hand and held it tightly.

The gesture meant so much to her.

The Vicar prayed for all those overseas fighting the war, for the casualties and the bereaved relatives and finally for the speedy conclusion of the conflict and a heartfelt 'Amen' rose from the congregation.

10

They saw one another as often as they could. James had not yet heard when he would be leaving.

'They take their time making decisions,' he said, but Nancy knew that he would have to go eventually and she tried not to think about that day.

James had paid another month's rent on the house and would continue to live there till he left. At first, his kisses were light and casual, usually when they met and when they parted, but one night, after James had visited Greystones, they stood in the darkened doorway and he took her in his arms and kissed her passionately.

'Nancy, Nancy,' he murmured against her hair, 'I think I am falling in love with you. Is that possible? I've never felt this way before. It was so different with . . .' he paused as if unable to mention the other Nancy's name, then continued, 'Nancy was always so volatile. She comes from a very wealthy background and she had been terribly spoilt.

'At first it amused me to spoil her as well, but that soon palled. And yet . . . and yet,' it was as though now he had started talking about her he couldn't stop, 'when we were apart I was miserable. She was like a powerful drug to me but now I can see that I had never really been in love with her.'

He paused and touched Nancy's face. 'Can that be called love, my Nancy, my second Nancy? My special Nancy. I believe we were meant to meet on that train. I believe we were meant to meet again, here at Greystones.'

He kissed her again, then smiled ruefully.

'My silent Nancy, too,' he teased. 'Why don't you say something?'

She laughed. 'You've hardly given me time, James.'

'I'm giving you time now,' he said gently.

She put her arms around his neck and whispered to him, 'I love you, too, James, I think I have always loved you from the moment we met.'

There, she had said it now. Once more they kissed and only broke away when someone came up the drive towards the house.

The news James had been waiting for came at last. He was to go to London on the 24th January.

It was too soon, Nancy thought desperately.

James said, 'I'm to work in an office, Nancy, poring over maps and plans. Apparently my eyesight is up to that, but not to going back to France.'

She knew he was disappointed, but secretly she herself was glad. She didn't want James to have to fight. True, there would be danger from bombs in London, too, but surely not the same danger. There would be shelters and sirens and lots of sandbags. That could not be compared with battle at the Front.

James asked her to go with him. 'You can be a nurse in London,' he said, 'just as easily as here.'

She was torn between her love for James and her loyalty to her Aunt Helen who depended on her, as she did on the rest of her staff. James misinterpreted her hesitation.

'I'd make sure you were safe, Nancy,' he said. 'You could live in the suburbs perhaps.' He smiled. 'I could find you some respectable lodgings with another Mrs Horsfall to keep her eye on you.'

Nancy thought about Mr Plummer and his kindly wife who she had met on several occasions. She could lodge with them, she was sure. She did not think Mr Plummer would be serving in the forces, he was much too old.

'I'd have to have a word with Aunt Helen first,' she said.

'Of course. I wouldn't dare make a move without Matron's blessing.'

Nancy began to feel excited. There must be a hospital somewhere that would take her on.

'And when this ghastly war is over we can get married,' James announced.

Her heart fluttered. 'Is that what you want?'

He gave her a little shake. 'No, I want to live in sin with you. Of course I want us to get married.' He suddenly looked worried. 'Why, would you turn me down? Is it because of Nancy? Don't you trust me?'

For answer she threw her arms around his neck and kissed him. 'Of course I trust you, silly! Yes, we'll get married.'

If only this could happen now. Tomorrow, Nancy thought impulsively, but there were other considerations. James' new job, her own career. Their country needed them both and when they finally did get married, it would have to be at the right time and in the right place.

And, surely, the war must be over soon.

Aunt Helen was always very busy, but Nancy got the opportunity to talk in private to her within a couple of days. Going to her private sitting-room where a cheery fire burned and the wireless was playing soft dance music.

'I've been expecting you coming to see me,' Aunt Helen said, smiling at Nancy and urging her to sit down by the fire.

'You have?' Nancy asked.

'It's to do with Captain Wallace, isn't it?'

Nancy nodded. 'He's leaving in a couple of weeks time.'

'I know that, Nancy.'

Of course she did. It was her business to know what happened to her 'boys' when they finally left her.

'Well, James wants me to go with him,' Nancy blurted out the words.

'And do you want to go?'

'Yes, I do, but I'm all in a muddle. Is it too soon, Aunt Helen? James was heartbroken when his fiancée deserted him, and that was such a short time ago. Now he says he loves me.'

'Do you love him?'

'Oh, yes, yes I do, with all my heart.'

It was only just now, in front of her aunt that Nancy had voiced or even thought of her concerns about James' declaration of love. Because it was what she had wanted to hear, she had pushed aside any idea that perhaps James was coming to her on the rebound. No, she wouldn't think that, even now! She was sure of him, of his feelings for her and hers for him.

'And so you want my blessing, Nancy?' Aunt Helen asked.

'More than that, I need to know you will let me go. I'm so happy here, Aunt Helen, I've enjoyed working with you.'

'And I with you, my dear. You will go far, I'm sure in your chosen career. I take it you will carry on working?'

'Oh, yes, we shan't think of marrying till the war is over.'

Aunt Helen nodded. 'I think that's wise,' she said. 'But Nancy, I must tell you something now, something you didn't know about me. When I was much younger, during the First World

War in fact, I was working in a hospital in Lancashire. There was a young army officer, much like your James.'

Nancy was pleased that Captain Wallace had now become 'her James'. 'He came to us as a war casually. Oh, he wasn't too seriously wounded, but he needed to be patched up. Well, to cut a long story short, we fell in love and when my soldier was discharged from hospital, he asked me to marry him.

'Of course, eventually he would have to go back to the Front, but like yourself and James we would probably have waited till the war was over to get married. But, Freddie, that was his name, wanted a commitment from me. A not unreasonable thing to ask, was it, Nancy, if I professed to love him. And I was sure I did, but I let him leave without me because I had become settled in my life at that particular hospital, promotion was just around the corner, and I didn't want to lose out on that.'

She paused and Nancy sat spell-bound waiting to hear more.

'So I told him 'No' and we went our separate ways. I never heard from him again and to this day I don't know what happened to him. Did he fall in battle? Did he live and marry someone else? Did they have children? All the things that have been denied me because I never again met anyone else I could love and there isn't a day goes by, even after all this time, that I don't think about Freddie or regret my action, or rather my inaction.'

So now Nancy knew why her aunt had never got married. She had often wondered why such a good looking woman, so sweet and gentle had remained single, and had presumed it was because she had put her career first and had never had the time for love. Well, in a way, she had been right.

Now she moved and kissed her aunt's cheek. 'Thank you for telling me your story, Aunt Helen,' she said.

Her aunt smiled. 'Has my story

helped you make up your mind? I shall be sorry to lose you, of course, but I give my blessing willingly.'

Suddenly there were tears in Nancy's eyes.

Only a couple of weeks left before they went to London. Nancy had already written to Mr Plummer and received a long letter back, giving her all his news. He had joined the Home Guard and his wife was working for the WRVS in Kingston.

The town had so far escaped any direct bombing and Randalls store was proudly and bravely continuing to serve its many loyal customers despite having lost most of its young male employees to the armed forces and some of the younger women who had signed up for the women's services or had gone to work as Land Girls. Randalls had always had a policy of employing older people in its store and now this stalwart band 'kept the flag flying' as Mr Plummer put it.

Of course you must come to us,

Nancy, he wrote in his letter. *Mrs Plummer and I will be delighted to have you. As for your finding work as a nurse here, I'm convinced that will not be difficult.*

So it was all arranged. James had already been told where he would be lodging and they would be able to see one another quite often, something that made Nancy feel very humble, knowing that so many women's sweethearts and husbands were overseas.

She walked down to the lakeside house one sunny afternoon. The snow had gone though it was still very cold. Mrs Horsfall came and opened the door to her.

'Miss Nancy,' she greeted with a beaming smile.

She had confessed to Nancy that she had never called 'that stuck up little madam' Miss Nancy, but only 'Miss Glenister' and that only in a disapproving tone.

As they went inside however, the housekeeper's voice dropped. 'I think the Captain is feeling a bit low today, Miss Nancy.'

'Oh?' Nancy's forehead creased into a worried frown.

Mrs Horsfall nodded. 'He's had a letter. Came this morning and since I gave it to him I've only seen him once. He popped his head round the sitting-room door and said 'I don't want any lunch, Mrs Horsfall.' Just like that, and there I'd bothered to make him a nice suet pudding.'

'Never mind,' Nancy said brightly, 'I'll cheer him up,' but still she was concerned as to who the letter was from and what it contained.

She found James sitting staring out of the window. His glasses were lying on a table by his side and Nancy knew he wouldn't be able to see very far without them.

'Hello, James,' she greeted going and kissing his cheek.

It may have been her imagination but it felt as though he was pulling away from her.

She sat on the settee. 'Is something wrong?' she asked, her eyes settled on the folded sheet of paper beside the glasses on the table.

'I can't go through with it, Nancy,' he said and his voice was low and hollow.

She suddenly felt sick inside. 'Through with what?'

Still he didn't bother to look at her. 'Us. I thought I could but now I realise it was too soon. I'm sorry, Nancy, I hate myself for feeling this way, but I can't help it. I want to be honest with you.'

His face turned towards her then and she saw the tears in his eyes, 'and I do love you, don't ever doubt that, you're a wonderful, wonderful person, but I don't deserve you. If I can feel like this, I don't deserve you. I would only make you very unhappy and I won't do that.'

'Is it because of the letter you received?' Nancy asked in a low, sickened voice.

Her heart had started to thump.

James picked up the sheet of paper, staring down at what was written there.

'It's from Nancy's parents. They're writing to tell me that Nancy has been killed. In a road accident in Washington. David Rattigan, too. They felt I should know, but I wish they hadn't told me. In time I'm sure I could have forgotten all about her. I could have had a better life with you, Nancy. We could have got married. Now . . . now . . . ' his voice broke off, choking with sobs.

Nancy wanted to comfort him, to put her arms around him, but she couldn't. She was too hurt, too stunned by his words.

Instead she said, 'But why should it change things between us, James, if we still love one another and we do, don't we? I'm very sorry about Nancy, but . . . '

James' expression stopped her in her tracks.

'Don't you understand? She's gone. That bright, vivacious, sparkling girl has gone. Oh, she made my life hell at times and yes, I know she deserted me, but she's dead, Nancy. And the pain has started all over again, but much, much worse this time.' He scrubbed at his eyes but the tears continued to fall.

And Nancy knew that it was over between them. In time, as James had said, he would have forgotten his ex-fiancée, she, Nancy would have helped him to do this. Their new life together would have been full and complete, but now ... now Nancy Glenister's ghost would always come between them, and even if James turned to her now and declared his undying love for her, she couldn't go through with it.

He belonged to the other Nancy, as he had in the past. He could never truly be hers.

11

It had been meant as a short break, a change of scenery to help her come to terms with what had happened, but it wasn't turning out like that.

It was Aunt Helen who had suggested she go back to Hepplestone.

'And leave you short-staffed?' Nancy had said.

'But I would have been without you, Nancy, dear, if you'd gone to London with James. I've got Nurse Riding arriving next week. Oh, she's very young, almost no experience of working with army personnel, but she's intelligent and very willing.'

Idiotically Nancy felt a twinge of jealousy, but Aunt Helen was right, she needed to get away. Wherever she walked in Greystones she could see James there, hear his voice, see his smile. She had to get him out of her system, go on with her life without him. Otherwise she would destroy herself and everyone else around her.

A nurse who was caring for wounded men, some of them only boys, some scared, some haunted by terrible visions, needed to be in control of herself. She needed to offer comfort, not receive it; she needed to sit sometimes for hours and listen to them talk, to hold their hands perhaps. It was not good for them, and certainly not for herself, if she felt like bursting into tears and running out of the ward.

So she went home. She packed only a small suitcase.

'Keep in touch, Nancy,' Aunt Helen said kindly, 'and when you feel like coming back just turn up on the doorstep.'

Because of the petrol shortage, she didn't take her car, the old car that had belonged to her father, but left that at Greystones and travelled by train. It was a long journey, with several changes and late into the evening when she finally arrived at York station.

She was pleased to see old Alfred Taylor was still plying his trade as a taxi driver outside the station. He recognised her at once.

'Miss Mellor!' he greeted, grinning at her. 'Home on leave, are you?'

'Something like that,' Nancy told him.

She knew of old that Alfred wouldn't need her to respond to his one-sided conversation and she sat in the back of the dark cab and let his pleasant northern voice drift over her, only occasionally catching what he said.

His favourite topic, of course, was the war, in particular The Enemy, as he now called the Germans. It was obvious he read every newspaper and listened avidly to the wireless. When he drew up outside the dark, empty house he made one final remark.

'Pity about Dr Bentley.'

Nancy stared at him. She had not been looking forward to meeting Alec again, but had fully expected him still to be there, running the surgery as he had said he would.

'What about him?' she asked.

'He's been killed in action.'

'But he was a doctor, not a soldier!'

Alfred nodded sagely. 'Aye, that's right, and he enlisted as a doctor. Nice chap, one of the best. 'I've got to join up, Alfred,' he once told me, 'I couldn't live with myself if I didn't'. But he was hit by a stray bullet, apparently, outside his field hospital, and that was that. He was a gonner.' He paused and stared at her, a worried look on his wrinkled face, 'Are you all right, lass?'

'Yes, thank you, I'm fine.' She paid Alfred, giving him a generous tip and let herself into the house.

It was very cold and had a musty smell. No longer the kindly Mrs Hedges there to greet her, no warm fire and clean sheets on the bed.

She couldn't take it in that Alec was dead. It seemed that the whole world was collapsing around her. Then she remembered the present he had sent

161

her at Christmas, which still remained unopened. In fact, for some reason she couldn't fathom, she had put it in the bottom of her suitcase.

She drew the curtains and the blinds and put the lights on, grateful that she had not had the electricity and gas turned off when she left. A friend of Mrs Hedges had been coming in to clean and despite the musty smell, Nancy could see that she had not neglected her duties. Nancy had left her enough money in advance so that she could buy whatever cleaning materials she needed and pay herself a generous wage.

Of course, it had been Nancy's intention, especially once James came into her life, to one day sell the house, but now . . . Well, she did not know in what direction her future would lie.

She went upstairs and put her suitcase on the bed, opening it immediately, feeling under her folded clothes for the garishly wrapped gift. She had not paid any particular attention to the brown paper in which it had arrived, but now saw that the words on the green and gold holly sprigged paper were in French, *Joyeux Noel*. Tiny intricate writing.

She sat on the bed and opened the paper. Inside was a gaudy coloured silk scarf. Alec must have taken the time and trouble to buy and post this gift to her and she had received it with scant attention. And the awful thing was that soon after this he must have been killed.

It was too much for her. Nancy burst into tears, sitting there with her head in her hands until she realised that the scarf was soaked with her tears.

She quickly smoothed it out and studied its rainbow colours carefully.

Dear, sweet Alec. They had had their ups and downs in the past and though she had been fond of him, she could never have loved him the way she loved James.

Now both men were gone from her life. Her future seemed bleak, but at least she had a future, she was alive, she was healthy and strong. She was a nurse! And no matter what she decided to do, she would always be able to practice her profession and help others.

It was amazing how quickly time passed. Days turned into weeks and weeks into months and gradually, Nancy discovered the new path she wanted to take.

She removed the dust covers from the furniture, she helped Mrs Armitage give everything an extra spit and polish, ensuring the good woman that doing this in no way reflected on the care that had been lavished on the house during her absence.

She got in touch with Mrs Hedges and discovered she was hale and hearty and enjoying her retirement.

She went down to the surgery where her father had practiced for so many years and Alec Bentley for only a short time, thrilled to find that old Dr Farnsworth had come out of retirement for the duration of the war.

He looked just the same as she remembered him from her childhood, greeting her warmly, commiserating with her over Alec's death.

'A fine man and a good doctor,' he said. 'I tried to talk him out of enlisting but he was determined.'

'And now you've stepped into his shoes,' Nancy said quietly.

Dr Farnsworth smiled, 'Well, I wouldn't go so far as to say that,' he said. Nancy knew the people of Hepplestone would be in good hands.

'And what of you, Nancy?' the doctor asked her, smiling at her across his desk. 'I understand you're working in the Lake District. A military convalescent home.'

'Yes.' Nancy decided not to tell Dr Farnsworth the whole truth. 'I'm on indefinite leave at the moment. Some personal matter.' She looked down at her hands.

'I see.' He didn't probe further and Nancy knew he never would. He wasn't that sort of person.

'But, my dear Nancy, I'm quite sure you won't want to idle your time away for too long.' His voice was hearty.

'I . . . I thought I might approach the Leeds General Infirmary where I did my training.' As Nancy spoke those words she finally admitted to herself that she would not be returning to Greystones.

Until now it had not been a conscious decision and she felt terribly guilt that she would be deserting her aunt. She had already worked in two nursing establishments and she really did not want to become a drifter, going from job to job. But she consoled herself by remembering that these were special times, there was a war on, people went where they were needed, did what they were needed to do.

'That's too bad,' Dr Farnsworth said slowly.

Nancy gave him a sharp glance. His eyes were fixed on her face. 'Sorry?' she queried.

'Oh, I'm sure the LGI would

welcome you with open arms, Nancy, but there is other work you can do. Nearer to home so to speak.'

'Go on,' Nancy urged.

'I'm badly in need of a nurse. Our very capable District Nurse has joined the WRENS and so far no-one has filled the gap. It's demanding work, Nancy, long hours, poor pay, meeting all sorts of people. Well, you'll know what your father had to do as a country doctor. I'm not as young as I was and I would be most grateful and thrilled too, if you would come in with me.' He saw the look on her face and hurried on. 'In a temporary capacity if you would prefer it that way, of course.'

No, if she took him up on his offer she would not regard the position as temporary. She would remain with him for the duration of the war, just as she was sure Dr Farnsworth himself would not go back into retirement till the conflict was over.

'I've never done midwifery,' she said.

Dr Farnsworth laughed. 'It isn't just

about delivering babies, Nancy,' he said, 'though they do still come along war or no war. We have a midwife on hand as and when, but I have complete confidence in you, Nancy and I'm sure, given time, even helping to bring a new life into the world will not be beyond your skills.'

His faith in her helped to strengthen her own confidence. Here was the perfect answer. She could remain in the house, her days would be full and varied. She had no doubt that she would find the work exhausting, but surely no more exhausting than working shifts in the convalescent home.

Her thoughts swung on to Aunt Helen. She would need her approval, but was sure it would be given. Her Aunt knew just how difficult it would be for her to return to Greystones.

'I'll do it,' she said stoutly.

Dr Farnsworth surprised her by coming round the desk and embracing her. 'Oh, you don't know what a weight that is off my mind,' he declared.

And, so Nancy entered a new phase in her life.

Of course she was working amongst people she knew, friendly, obliging people who all had a good word for Dr John Mellor, and also for Dr Alec Bentley.

'So glad you've come back home, Nurse Mellor.'

'You're a godsend as I'm sure dear Dr Farnsworth has told you.'

These and other similar remarks were made to her all the time. Nancy felt fulfilled. Though, at the same time, she sometimes felt very lonely, especially at night when she was alone in the house.

Luckily the nights were lightening and spring was on the doorstep. Fresh shoots on trees and bushes, blue tits checking out the nesting box in the garden, as they did every year, the feel of the gradually warming sun on face and arms.

Sometimes it was so difficult to believe a war was still raging overseas, and not just overseas, London and the south east had had its share of bombs, of death and destruction. Even northern cities as near as Sheffield and Hull had also been targeted.

Hepplestone had made room in its heart and homes for a few evacuees who alone brought a new challenge to Dr Farnsworth and Nancy. Many were infected with head lice, generally thinner than the northern children, though wiry and strong, and yes, some were little horrors, pinching vegetables, mainly podded peas, playing truant from the village school and using every opportunity they could to run wild. But they had a wistful charm, too, a ready word, some that Nancy would not have cared to repeat, friendly and obliging in their own way. Nancy knew how hard it must be to have to leave their homes and families and live amongst strangers.

For the most part, she kept busy but there was never a day went by that James wasn't in her thoughts at some time or other.

How was he? Was he in danger? Had

he settled into his new job? Did he ever think of her? No-one knew that she held a young army captain in a special place in her heart. That she prayed for him every night; that she often shared the events of her day with him, talking softly into the darkness when she was in bed, knowing how foolish she was being, but unable to stop herself.

She wondered if it would always be like this. Surely time healed. Isn't that what they said? Surely when the war finally ended and life went back to something like normal she would be able to let James go, get on with her own life and not keep constantly wondering what he was doing with his.

12

It was a glorious day in early May, 1945. Glorious because of the weather, glorious because of victory in Europe, only dimmed a little perhaps by the knowledge that in the Far East the war continued and that many soldiers remained prisoners of the Japanese.

But in Hepplestone at least there was an air of rejoicing; the boys would be coming home! Some had fallen, it was true, including Alec Bentley and these brave men were well remembered, but for the sake of the children and the great sense of jubilation and euphoria in the small town, as everywhere else in Britain, a street party was held, with bunting flying, pictures of the King and Queen pasted into windows, black out curtains tossed aside, ongoing rationing forgotten for a while and everybody determined to have a good time.

Nancy made small iced buns and jellies and Mr Ginelli, an Italian immigrant who had lived in Hepplestone for many years, conjured up his own homemade ice-cream in the back of his tiny confectionery shop. The children laughed and danced, picking up the excitement of their elders and it was growing dark before the festivities finally began to wind down.

Dr Farnsworth joined Nancy on a bench by the side of the green where long trestle tables had been set up and the local pub was still doling out drinks, turning a blind eye to the lateness of the hour.

'Well, Nancy,' he said with a smile, 'peace at last. Doesn't it feel good?'

Nancy nodded. 'It certainly does,' she said.

'And now I shall be able to go back to my gardening and my fishing I expect.' The doctor spoke with a wistful tone in his voice.

'Straight away?'

'Perhaps not as quickly as that, but I

only took on the job for the duration. That was always understood. A much younger man than I is needed here. It's a very large practice. And what about you, Nancy? Will you stay here?'

'I think so. I was born here.'

'And you intend to keep on nursing?'

'Of course.' His question surprised her.

'I just wondered if you might not want to get married one day, settle down and have children.'

He had touched a raw nerve and he saw this at once. He put his hand on her arm lightly. 'Forgive an old fool, Nancy dear, it's really none of my business. I apologise.'

But it hadn't been an unreasonable question she realised. 'There was someone once.' She spoke the words quickly before she could change her mind.

'Here in Hepplestone?' A look of shock crossed his face. 'Not Alec Bentley? Oh, my dear, I'm so sorry. I had no idea . . . '

Nancy smiled. 'It wasn't Alec. Oh, perhaps a few years ago before the war he and I were more than just good friends but it didn't last and we parted mutually. No, it was someone I met in the Lake District.'

'A soldier?'

'Yes.'

'So you nursed him back to health. Is that it?'

'In a way, yes, but something happened. Oh, he wasn't killed or anything like that. It was just that . . . ' Nancy was beginning to regret starting down that road.

'I understand, my dear,' the doctor said softly. 'If it pains you, please don't say any more.' He glanced out across the green.

Women in flowered aprons and summer hats were starting to clear away the debris and men with rolled up shirt sleeves were dismantling the tables.

'At least the war is over, and when Japan surrenders . . . ' Dr Farnsworth's voice trailed off.

'Do you think they will?' Nancy asked, glad of a change of subject.

'I'm sure of it. I mean, it has to happen one day, in one way or another, hasn't it?'

Nancy hoped he was right. She didn't know a great deal about the Japanese people, only what she and countless others had gleaned from newspaper articles and the wireless, but they seemed a stubborn race, spurning what they perceived as weakness, wanting to win whatever the cost to them or to others, even though Germany had surrendered unconditionally.

'We shall just have to leave it to our good friends the Americans, I suppose,' Dr Farnsworth said, with a faint trace of sarcasm in his voice. He stood up. 'Well, Nancy, I'm for my last pipe of the day and a good strong mug of tea.' He held out his hand and Nancy shook it. 'I'll more than likely see you around.'

Of course, he would still be Hepplestone's doctor till a replacement could be found, and she would be working alongside him as she had for the past three years. It was not an unwelcome prospect.

It was a few weeks later. Summer was here, there were lambs in the fields, flowers in the hedgerows. Nancy had finished a long stint at the bedside of a young woman who eventually gave birth to a fine healthy little boy. Dr Farnsworth had been right, she had added midwifery to her skills.

The woman smiled proudly, her face glistening with perspiration. 'My Donald will be that chuffed,' she said, cradling her dark haired son in her arms. 'Just think, if he hadn't come home on that compassionate leave because of his poor mam, we wouldn't have little Michael John would we?' Then she covered her mouth with her hand and blushed. 'Oops,' she said embarrassed.

'Does your husband know about the baby?' Nancy asked.

'Oh, yes, I've written to him. I tell you, he'll be chuffed! He'll be home soon, any road. This demob business takes its time!'

Nancy left the little cottage shortly afterwards. It had surprised her how many babies had come along during the war. Soldiers on leave, farmers and their helpers in reserved occupations, life went on, as Dr Farnsworth was always reminding her.

One of the requisites of being a district nurse had been the ability to ride a bicycle, a skill Nancy had neglected in her later years, but it was true what they said. You never forgot how to ride a bike!

On this particular afternoon she rode along the leafy lanes back to the house. It was impossible to be unhappy and, indeed, she had a great deal for which to be thankful.

As Poplar House came into view she started to slow down, the house was set in a slight hollow and freewheeling would be sufficient to take her down the lane.

She had found since coming home

that she liked gardening which was perhaps as well as there was a large garden to take care of. Nancy didn't have any help in the house but preferred to look after it herself. It meant she was mostly kept busy without a great deal of spare time in which to brood.

Suddenly a man came into view around the corner of the house as though he had been walking around the garden. He was tall, dark-haired, wearing a white shirt, open at the neck and a pair of light-coloured trousers.

Nancy turned into the driveway and saw that it was James. She brought the bicycle to an abrupt halt and dropped her feet to the ground.

He saw her and started to walk down the drive. Nancy's hands gripped the handlebars.

'Hello, Nancy,' he greeted.

He still wore his thick lensed glasses. His hair was much longer than she remembered and his expression was solemn.

'Hello, James,' she said.

She felt weak at the knees. The weeks and months fell away as she looked into the eyes of the man she loved who had occupied so many of her dreams. Nothing had changed, for her nothing ever would. But why was he here?

'I was looking at your garden,' James said next. 'It's very lovely.'

'How did you know where to find me?' Nancy asked, still standing astride her bicycle.

James smiled for the first time. 'From your Aunt Helen, of course. I telephoned her.'

Nancy didn't know whether to be angry or pleased with her aunt for divulging this information.

'And just why are you here, James?' she asked next.

'To see you, of course.' He spoke simply as though their last meeting when he was weeping tears over the other Nancy had never taken place.

'You'd better come in,' she said, pushing her bicycle past him, leaning it against the side of the house.

'Still wearing a uniform, I see,' James said in a joking voice.

For some reason his lightness irritated her. She turned on him.

'And you're not, I see. Is that because the war is over or because you are no longer a serving soldier?'

He looked down at his feet. 'I've left the army,' he told her. 'As soon as peace was declared, though I'd had it in mind to do so for some time. I was never going to be able to serve as I would wish to, in any war, my eyes won't ever be any better than they are now. If I was going to do a desk job I decided it might as well be in civvy street. That's what my father always had planned for me, anyway. He's a solicitor.'

It was the first time James had discussed his family. Somehow she couldn't see him working as a solicitor.

It even felt odd his not wearing a uniform, he looked uncomfortable to her, out of place somehow, but if that was his decision . . . And, anyway, what did it have to do with her?

They went into the house. Nancy took James into the sitting-room and went to put the kettle on, but when she turned from the stove, he was standing in the doorway, watching her.

She felt flustered and asked him, 'Are you staying around here?'

'Yes. At the Red Lion. I may as well be honest, Nancy, I'm coming to live in York, that's where I intend to practice law.'

'You're a qualified solicitor?'

'Not quite.' He smiled again and her heart melted. 'I was an article clerk in my father's firm till I decided to become a regular soldier. It was always a bone of contention between us and he's over the moon that I've decided to pick up where I left off. I've been accepted into a small firm in York and I shall be given day release to study and evening classes too, so you see I shall be kept busy and out of mischief.'

'Why did you choose York, James?'

she asked him when the silence became unbearable.

'Can't you guess, Nancy?'

She knew he had come to stand just behind her, so close that if she turned she would be in his arms, and she couldn't allow that to happen so she spoke with her back to him.

'James, you must go. This isn't doing either of us any good.' She felt his hands on her arms and still not looking at him, dragged herself free and fled to the other side of the kitchen, the tea forgotten.

His hands dropped to his sides

'Do you know I would rather have faced a line of German soldiers any day than come here today, Nancy, but I had to, because I love you. I've never stopped loving you. I was a fool, a stupid fool and I'm sorry I hurt you so badly.'

She held her breath. Her head told her to scream at him to go away and leave her alone and never come back, but her heart wouldn't let her. She wanted so much to kiss him, to feel his arms around her, but she had to be strong. Nancy Glenister would always stand between them.

'Do you remember that day on the train when we first met?' James asked in a gentle voice.

As if she could ever forget. She didn't answer him and he went on.

'Let's go back to that day, Nancy. Let's start all over again. I am free now, I know that, I swear by all I hold dear that I am free. The world, too, is free from the grip of tyranny. It's a new beginning for thousands of people, so let it be a new beginning for us, Nancy. No war can part us, no treachery can keep us apart. I'll court you, as I should, I'll bring you flowers, I'll take you dancing. Do you remember how we danced on Christmas Eve in that house by the lake?'

'Yes, I remember.' Despite herself Nancy felt a tremor of excitement.

'Well, I'm no Fred Astaire, but I believe I have a left and a right foot.'

The smile came again. 'I'll work hard, I'll make you proud of me, Nancy. I promise you. We won't be rushed. After all, we have all the time in the world. Just give me a chance. That's all I ask. One more chance.'

Could she do it? She wanted to, oh how she wanted to.

James started to walk towards her and she didn't flee from him. He leaned forward and kissed her, only on the cheek but it was enough.

'I love you, Nancy.' Simple words.

'I love you, James.' Her words, too, were simple.

THE END

We do hope that you have enjoyed reading this large print book.

Did you know that all of our titles are available for purchase?

We publish a wide range of high quality large print books including:
Romances, Mysteries, Classics
General Fiction
Non Fiction and Westerns

Special interest titles available in large print are:
The Little Oxford Dictionary
Music Book, Song Book
Hymn Book, Service Book

Also available from us courtesy of Oxford University Press:
Young Readers' Dictionary
(large print edition)
Young Readers' Thesaurus
(large print edition)

For further information or a free brochure, please contact us at:
Ulverscroft Large Print Books Ltd.,
The Green, Bradgate Road, Anstey,
Leicester, LE7 7FU, England.
Tel: (00 44) 0116 236 4325
Fax: (00 44) 0116 234 0205